T0271737

Dead Animals

Phoebe Stuckes is a writer from West Somerset living in London. Her writing has appeared in *The Poetry Review*, *The Rialto*, *The North* and *Ambit* among others. She was commended by the UEA New Forms Award and shortlisted for the PFD Agents Queer Fiction Prize in 2022. *Dead Animals* is her first novel.

Dead Animals

Phoebe Stuckes

sceptre

First published in Great Britain in 2024 by Sceptre
An imprint of Hodder & Stoughton
An Hachette UK company

2

A CIP catalogue record for this title is available from the British Library

Hardback ISBN 9781399728133
ebook ISBN 9781399728157

Typeset in Sabon MT Std by Manipal Technologies Limited.

Printed and bound in Great Britain by Clays Ltd, Elcograf S.p.A.

Hodder & Stoughton policy is to use papers that are natural, renewable and recyclable products and made from wood grown in sustainable forests. The logging and manufacturing processes are expected to conform to the environmental regulations of the country of origin.

Hodder & Stoughton Ltd
Carmelite House
50 Victoria Embankment
London EC4Y 0DZ

www.sceptrebooks.co.uk

For J.J., who holds me up when I am heavy.

At the end of my suffering
there was a door

— Louise Glück

Prologue

Here's the thing about getting hit: sometimes you don't remember if you asked him to do it or not. Or if you did ask, you must not have asked for it to be that hard. *No one would ask for that*, you think, you wouldn't want someone to notice in the morning when you were sober and tired and on your way to shower at home with all your own products. You don't want to be looked at with pity by strangers, by anyone. When you ask to be hit you want him to at least be a little reluctant. Like he can't bear to hit you, but he'll do it because you asked and he knows it turns you on. As it is, he doesn't behave that way at all. He acts like a dog let off a leash, you can feel his rabid excitement. His enjoyment is derived not from seeing how the slap turns you on, but from the cringe of your body in pain. You realise this when he follows up the first slap with a second and a third. You remember being unsure if the third hit could even be classified as a slap. You remember little else.

Your body documents it for you, the smears of dried brown blood on your thighs.

'Oh, did you get your period?' he asks casually in the morning, he wants to show you he can say the word period, that it doesn't scare him.

You laugh nervously, this is the default sound you make, you don't actually *say* anything. You reach up to rub your eye but when you touch it, it is hot and enlarged, *Why is it hot and enlarged?* you think. In the bathroom mirror your lip is swollen and bruised. All you can think about is leaving the house like that, what will your friends say, how will you explain it? There is nothing to be done. It feels like your mistake, like maybe you fell down the stairs, maybe you slipped and hit the coffee table, maybe you got in a fight you don't remember. Your body catalogues more information, there are large floral bruises on your side, your arms, your legs. You don't know what to do, so you take out your phone and take pictures, you will think about this later, you decide, you will think about this later, maybe never, maybe you will never think about this again.

Leaving the flat is not difficult, because by this point your mind is on another plane, maybe you make excuses, maybe you just pick up your things and leave. You can't remember which of these things you do, because you know he is indifferent to your presence by this point and all you are thinking about is being outside and walking away from the building that contains his flat. Walking away and forgetting what it looked like, where it was, what the street was called. You remember the vague sense that somewhere there would be a train station, and if you got on a train and maybe two or three more you could end up back at your place and lock the door. That your flat would wrap its arms around you, and no one else could get in. Not for the first time you wish you had a bathtub, there would be something healing, baptismal even, in immersing yourself in water, if only you were rich enough to live somewhere with a bathtub, if only the bathroom wasn't shared with the other people on your floor.

By the time you are home you have only the faintest sense of how you got there. The door closes behind you and it's as if you have woken up. You don't understand this phenomenon, this forgetting that has nothing to do with alcohol or injuries. These gaps in time. It is dark by the time you realise you are in the shower. The sky is gorgeous and wrong, deep blue streaked with pink. Your whole body has become cold on the walk, the hot water is painful. The water gets into all the places where you hurt, you sting and ache. You want to understand the bruises but you can't, there are scratches you didn't notice in your first assessment, in private and soft places – the underside of your forearms. It's like you've survived a horror, it's as if you've crawled through the woods.

You slowly turn the tap to make the water cold, to force yourself to get out, you rub moisturiser methodically into the dry parts of your skin, you look at yourself in the mirror. You recognise the little crease in your forehead, your tensed jaw is twitching a little, you try to relax your face and shoulders. You have a horrible thought: with a face like this you can't go to work, you imagine being sent home from the catering shift because of your banged-up face and for a second feel a sadness so physical a searing pain develops in your brow bone.

*

You are in the crisps and snacks aisle in Sainsbury's, several weeks later, when a section of the evening crashes over your head. *I said no.* The words come to you so fast it's as if someone else has said them to you. You remember sitting on the sofa, the fabric felt itchy on your legs, you were too drunk to get up.

The man at the party was incredibly handsome, so handsome that his interest in you felt like a joke. He had been staring at you all night with an intensity you found interesting and annoying in equal measure. It reminded you of the way strange men look at you on the tube sometimes, they eye you like crocodiles in a glass tank. He was on his way over to you before you noticed, you said no, you protested, you had excuses, then a whole lot of nothing, then a series of events you struggle to name. You open your mouth and then close it again.

I got obsessed with thinking I was in the wrong place at the wrong time. Everything felt *wrong*, wrongness had settled over me and everything I touched. At my job, I was always doing the wrong thing, folding napkins when I should have been clearing tables, clearing tables when there was hot food waiting to be brought to customers. I was working as a waitress in a very expensive restaurant in Knightsbridge, a job that was supposed to be somewhat prestigious. It was called *Veau*, as in Veal. Their specialism was pieces of offal and octopus served on plates so large it hurt my wrists to pick them up. It used to take me an hour to get there, one regular train, two different underground lines. I was permanently exhausted. It didn't occur to me to get a job closer to my flat, to do something else, the thought of finding a new job, learning the processes of a new restaurant all over again made me nauseous. At least at Veau I knew how everything worked. It was a brutal regime, the chefs didn't like it when we brought our water glasses into the kitchen, we used to hide pint glasses of tap water all over the restaurant. Sometimes one of us, usually Eva, would notice that there were too many hidden and clear them all away and the process of sneaking away to fill a glass and hide it would begin all over again.

*

When I was short on shifts I would take extra work with this faceless, silver service catering company. I was always telling myself there are worse jobs. The events always felt strange, I would get transported into the middle of a stranger's wedding or family party or huge glitzy corporate do. I would hover in the background of the most important night of someone else's life, wan and hungry. Because the shifts were long and the hours were strange, I was always hungry. Carting around the plates of roast beef or trays of canapés made it worse, the smells kept me up at night, by turns intoxicating and repulsing me. My most useful skill was that I always remembered what was in the canapés: *roasted tomato arancini with basil aioli, roasted pork belly with salted caramel jus, parma violet mousse in a miniature ice cream cone with popping candy and edible flowers.* If the clients didn't eat everything, the managers made us throw the leftovers away. At one of the corporate events no one touched the individual crèmes brûlées, perfectly set custard topped with a caramel shard. Me and two other girls whose names I don't remember clustered around the bin, digging the custard and caramel out of the ramekins with our fingers, surreptitiously shoving it in our mouths.

*

The managers were always telling me my appearance was all wrong. My shirts in particular were never up to their standards. I tried to tell them I didn't own an iron, that I had nowhere to hang the shirt up, but they didn't care. After that I used to hang up my shirt in the bathroom when I showered, hoping it would steam the wrinkles out. I would wake up on my days off, certain there was a shift I was supposed to do that I'd forgotten. That someone was going to ring me angrily and tell me I was late. When I went to sleep the night before a shift I kept checking my alarm, certain it wouldn't go off and I'd be in trouble again.

*

I felt by turns conspicuous and invisible. When I was wearing the same as all the other girls on the shift, I could have been anyone. I made no effort when I got ready for work, I didn't wear makeup, I wasn't especially good-looking but I wasn't necessarily ugly either. I felt profoundly average. I wasn't thin, no matter how much I starved on those shifts, I never lost any weight. I felt uncomfortable in all of my clothes. Sometimes it was like my whole body was covered in insects, sometimes my body was like a heavy suitcase I had to haul around. I often found myself standing with a heavy tray, a piece of slate, a china plate, a novelty wicker basket, repeating myself, waiting for someone to notice me:

'Would you like a . . . canapé? Champagne?'

*

Eva was a full-time waitress at Veau. She noticed me trying to fit in, she saw me one night, dialling up the posh notes in my voice, speaking louder, clearer, I made the whole table laugh when I cracked a joke.

'Psychopath,' she hissed at me as she walked past. I wondered if she was right. I got called so many other names: *excuse me, hey you, would you mind?* On the catering shifts it was even worse, the chefs called me sweetheart, darling, the terms of endearment braised in sarcasm. Sometimes they'd make an effort, ask our names at the start of the shift, and then they'd spend the rest of the shift mixing us up. I had been Constance, Chloe, Sophie, even Katie. I wondered who these women were, the women they'd see in their minds when they looked at me. I wanted to be them, I wanted to be them but better.

*

My peers couldn't understand it, they thought because I had been educated with them, I should have been able to find a better job. It hadn't been such a big deal, the disparity, when we were all at university and I couldn't afford to go on holiday. I stayed in our university town during the summers, I had various jobs, I waited patiently for September. When it finally rolled around it was like the person who had worked all summer had gone away again, had never really existed. I hid that person from my friends, but after graduating it was impossible to hide her anymore. My real life was different from theirs. I tried to tell them what it was like, but they didn't know, they couldn't, they refused to imagine.

'It's the boredom that's the killer,' I would say. The shifts where nothing happened, the shifts where I would lean against the wall, trying to lift some weight from my feet, trying to sleep with my eyes open. I thought I could make it sound funny, the lack of humanity could get bizarre, hilarious even. There was a week where I was on antibiotics for an infected wisdom tooth. I made small sandwiches of brown bread and honey and hid them in the fridge next to the tiny dishes that held fat coins of French butter.

'What the hell is this?' Cherie, my manager for the evening, asked, picking my sandwiches up exaggeratedly between her finger and thumb.

'I have to eat every four hours,' I explained, 'it's because of the antibiotics.' She rolled her eyes and threw my sandwich back in the fridge.

*

I was dislocated, I belonged to nothing, I didn't really exist. I would get back to my bedsit and not know exactly how

I'd got there. I tried to piece together the transport, which trains I could have got on. I tried to picture the faces of the other passengers on the tube but I came up with nothing, it was like fishing in your pockets for change and touching only fabric. I shrugged about it, I supposed if nothing happened that I could remember, then nothing bad could have happened. I guessed that if something bad had happened, then I would have remembered. My body was often frozen when I got in and it was difficult to get warm again. I used to run on the spot on my creaky floor, stand in the shower with the water turned up so hot it stung my scalp. It didn't work, my feet were always icy, my side was cold to the touch like a side of salmon. I became convinced I was getting ill but I never seemed to have time for appointments, that is, if I could get one. The hold music from the doctor's surgery seemed to go on forever, by the time it rang out it started again, it restarted a second time, on the third I heard that double tone that told me whoever was on the other end of the line had picked up the phone only to put it down again.

I came to and my friend Rosa was saying, 'You have to exercise.' *When the hell am I going to do that?* I thought, I figured if I didn't stop to think, everything would be fine. Rosa was convinced that I had chronic fatigue, post-viral fatigue, some kind of chronic illness. I suppose there were signs, the feeling of intense cold that sometimes washed over me, the prickly feeling across my skin, the nausea, the phantom period pains. They weren't connected to anything but were nonetheless agonising, they rose in great tides from my cervix until I leaned against the side of the walk-in freezer, spots in front of my eyes.

'I don't know,' I said to her, sighing, 'maybe my life is just exhausting.' Rosa tried to arrange her face sympathetically.

They didn't get it, these friends, they had office jobs, they had unstructured time, they sat down all day, how could they begin to understand?

*

The truth is you can never know how you will react when something like what happened to me happens to you. You will believe that you know yourself, that you are prepared for disaster but you aren't, you won't be.

*

All my shoes started to fall apart and I didn't understand why. I looked at my feet, wondering if they were so bony that they had shredded the inside of my shoes. Soon the shredded insides created big shaggy holes in my socks. I remember thinking, *this is awful*, when I put on another pair of black socks that had no heels. I had to go to Primark and get the cheapest multipacks I could find. I thought I would do this on my way to another waitering job in Holborn. I moved through the huge Primark, it smelled of newness, hot plastic, even the cheap packs seemed more expensive than I remembered so I abandoned the errand, put it off until another day when I could face it. I walked out determinedly, fast. When I got outside the venue I rummaged in my bag for my ID and there were packs and packs of socks, not just socks, a lipstick or two as well, a slimy faux-satin scrunchie. None of which I remembered touching. It was late, I didn't have time to think about how they got in there. I changed into my new socks in the bathroom of the corporate building. I decided I would just never go into that branch of Primark ever again.

*

In the long afternoons at the restaurant, when there was nothing to do, I would get obsessive about cleaning. I'd stack up the cups and saucers, so hot from the dishwasher they hurt my hands. I'd wipe up coffee grounds and polish butter knives with cloth napkins. I'd fill a plastic bucket with chemicals that made my head swim, I'd mop the chemicals into wet symbols on the wooden floor and obliterate them with a final sweep of the mop. I would do this until the floors shone wetly and the contents of the bucket were opaque with dirt. I'd fit half my body inside the glass-washer trying to clean it. Scum would come off the mesh insides in thick clumps and slough off into the plastic pail. I'd run more chemicals through the coffee machine. Everything in the kitchen was filled with dirt or poison. Nothing was ever exactly as clean as I wanted it to be. The floor was dirty when the surfaces were clean, there were no clean coffee cups when there were enough teaspoons.

It was so unsatisfying, but better than dealing with the customers. They filled me with anger, it felt hot and wet. Customers are a screaming hydra of need, they exist in a permanent state of want. Even when they didn't want anything, they wanted me to leave them alone. They wanted it so much. It hurt to say *no, I cannot leave your eye line, I'm sorry, I will be here, I have to be available.* They were suspicious of me, when I'd survey the dining room they'd catch my eye and frown or avoid my gaze irritably. They'd think I was eavesdropping on their conversations, because they didn't know how incredibly boring they were. When I started working at Veau I thought I might get something out of listening to people's dates, anniversaries, celebrations, but now I know most people's conversations are the same. They think you are storing up their information, filing it away in your dirty mind. They didn't know I would forget everything that happened in a shift as soon as I left, the evenings immediately slid from my grasp as soon as my coat was on. The exception, of course, was when something terrible would happen. The arguments varied endlessly and were always fascinating. I was desperate for conflict, plot, telenovela, accusations of infidelity, money trouble, petty jealousies. Even work talk can be interesting when someone is being dragged through the mud. I felt that if a man were to get into a conflict with his business partner and reach over the tablecloth and plunge the waiting steak knife into his stationary hand, me and the other waitresses would scream from the catharsis, the ecstasy. No such luck. As long as I was standing there I was a reminder that they could ask, demand, pay for whatever they wanted. I had my limits. I could only give so much, after a certain amount of time passed I had to fight to keep my face neutral, but the truth was I hated their guts.

The hatred stayed with me even when I left, when I joined the crowds flowing into the underground, I hated them too. I scowled at the sound of men singing football chants. Once on my way home, a teenage boy laughed and all I could think about was how badly I wanted to punch him, knock out his crooked tooth. There was nowhere for my hatred to go, I thought about accidents on oil rigs, fires that never die down, long tongues of toxic orange flame on top of cool water. My anger was only supposed to have one source, one font, one spring. After what happened it sprung up everywhere like damp, it was threatening to bring down the whole house. It infected my entire life. My friends noticed the looks on my face, the two settings I had: disgust and exhaustion. Hatred and the dark shadows under my eyes, the furrow in the centre of my forehead that threatened to become permanent. There was no getting away from it, I was simply not as fun as I used to be. I stopped going to events where I thought I would have to have fun. I was on thin ice when Rosa invited me to the party. It felt like my last chance, and besides I was bored. I had identified a new feeling: the blinding desire for something, anything, to happen. I had to be witnessed. Without this opportunity to wear makeup, dress up, wear my own clothes, I only existed at work and at work I could feel myself disappearing. I wanted to feel *different*.

*

Rosa was the only person I knew who was going to the party, it was all the way across town. I was in South London then, everyone I knew was at least forty-five minutes away. It wasn't as if I loved going to parties before, crowds always made me nervous. Recently I couldn't see any reason to put myself in any situation where my friends would be outnumbered by strangers, where the location was far away from an easy route home, where the location was someone else's house and not the cheap bar chain that we all used to go to back then. But I had something to prove. I wanted so badly to not be afraid, to do something normal. I might not have agreed to the party if there weren't hawthorn trees breaking into flower by the train station, or if my astrology app hadn't sent a notification telling me that it was a day for feeling *powerful* and *living up to your potential*. I have always been superstitious, I was holding on to any omens I could get. The memory of what happened seemed like it was crouched in my peripheral vision, ready to strike the minute I let my mind wander. I kept song lyrics in my head like mantras.

I thought if I could get the outfit right, the makeup right, listen to the right music, I could keep myself safe. I started getting ready too early. I forced myself to eat something light, soba noodles, soy sauce and green vegetables. When you work with food there are days when you want to eat everything and days when you want to eat nothing. I was a vegetarian so there was hardly anything on the restaurant menu I could eat, even the potatoes were soaked in dripping. The smells used to drive me wild, something primal and anaemic in me made the smell of searing steak addictive, I would find myself gnawing at my fingertips, drinking in the aroma until someone told me to move.

*

While I ate I liked to read articles about the failures of people richer and more powerful than me through my cracked phone screen. A company that rented out scooters in San Francisco had lost $10 million and wanted another $20 million to get going again. A twenty-seven-year-old man had organised a festival that left hundreds of rich twenty-somethings trapped in airports or on a deserted island with no tents, no mattresses, no sanitation. I loved that story, I read anything anyone had to say about it, any way they wanted to spin it, it was a consequence of social media, it was predicted by Baudrillard, it was the fault of those rich kids dumb enough to believe him. Everyone kept referring to the man who'd masterminded the whole mess as a *boy, just a young boy, boyishly handsome*. I saw his pudgy face everywhere, in every new window I opened. When he talked on video his eyes flicked from side to side in that coked-up way I recognised from the finance guys I used to meet sometimes in clubs. I was always thinking about how ridiculous he was. Even when he was out on bail he'd tried to run another scam, something about emails offering tickets for VIP events. He was always striving for something unattainable, trying to get into that special room where there were no limits, where nothing was out of reach, an invisible hand attending to everything, everything perfect and beautiful. I didn't get it. I didn't want any of that, I just wanted to relax.

I looked down and I'd run out of soba noodles, there was a little puddle of soy sauce and water where they'd been that I dumped down the sink. I wanted to wear a lot of makeup to the party, whenever I'd tried to wear it to work I just sweated it off. I wanted to dress up, look good. My makeup wouldn't do what I wanted it to. The eyeliner made my eyes look huge and vulnerable, like the smudged image of a cartoon deer. I got frustrated and sweaty. I took it all off and started again. None of my clothes fit me right, it was always a complicated game, trying to fit the outfit so my stomach looked flatter and my waist looked smaller. I briefly gave up, lay down on top of my duvet and contemplated cancelling. As if sensing my doubts Rosa sent me a message: I'll meet you outside! You won't have to walk in alone glitter emoji. I groaned.

*

15

The trains were all running late, I watched the minutes ticking up on the illuminated sign: *expected 20:20 20:21 20:22*. I was taking rapid sips from my bottle of cheap wine on the train platform, carefully screwing the lid back on and hiding it in the black plastic bag the off-licence gave me. I looked across the platform, the whole thing was lit up in that syrupy yellow, Transport for London light. Further along I could see a man sitting on a bench looking down at his phone. He looked familiar but I couldn't place where I'd seen him before. He turned his head slightly and I could see how his hair was shaved at the back of his head. I felt immediately sick, I panicked, was it him? I couldn't see his face from where I was standing. I tried to reason with myself, what would he be doing in this part of town anyway? I stared and stared until he looked up confused and caught my eye. It was a different man, he smiled nervously at me. I turned and walked further down the platform, into the dark, I wanted both of their faces out of my mind.

*

When the train arrived it made a discordant musical sound as it lurched back and forth over the tracks, like someone blowing tunelessly into a harmonica. My purse wasn't big enough to fit a book so I scrolled mindlessly through other people's thoughts and pictures, forgetting them as soon as I swiped past.

*

The station where I was supposed to get off was packed with people going to their own parties, tall men in chinos and peacoats, women with highlights and tall heels cackling. I hated and envied them at the same time. It wasn't as if any of them could have been me. I texted Rosa to tell her I would be there soon and followed the little blue dot across the map on my phone until I got to a house with all the lights on and music pulsing out. Various cool-looking people were standing outside the front, perched on the crumbling garden wall or slouched against the door frame, smoking and clutching each other. I couldn't see Rosa anywhere, it was colder than I thought when I had left the flat. I dropped my bag in the dim doorway but kept my coat on. It felt as if everyone turned to look at me when I walked into the living room. The light was blue, a song that felt hurtfully loud and vaguely familiar was playing. I felt a panic attack coming on, that painful yelping-feeling like a puppy scratching at a door, I could feel it getting higher and higher in my chest. My arms felt so cold and I didn't know why. The bathroom door wouldn't lock properly but the room was small enough that I could sit down on the toilet and jam one of my feet against the door. It couldn't completely drown out the music but it softened it slightly. I rested my forehead against the side of the sink and breathed hard but the deeper I breathed in the more panicked I felt, it was like no air was getting in. The blood drained out of my hands, I could feel them tingle, they looked so pale, like they belonged to someone else. Someone banged hard on the wooden door with the flat of their palm. I started in surprise.

'Can you let me in please?' The voice was clipped and supremely confident, it scared me immediately.

'I don't care if you're peeing!' she said. I ignored it, I was about to start crying and there were words in my head but my mouth wouldn't co-operate, my jaw was clenched so tight it could have been wired shut.

'Come on, I just need a tissue. I've got a nosebleed. I am *literally* covered in blood.'

I wondered who the voice was monologuing to. To my horror she pushed the door open, painfully shoving my foot out of the way with the door, I was still hyperventilating.

'Jesus,' she said exasperatedly. There was a spatter of blood that stretched from under her nostrils and dripped down over her top lip. She reached over and tore off some toilet roll, she turned on the tap to moisten the tissue and began to wipe away at the blood, wincing slightly as she did it. She bared her teeth into the mirror and the blood was there too in the gaps between her perfectly white teeth. She spat daintily into the sink, drank out of the tap, swilled it around and spat it out again. When she looked up again I could feel her looking at me in the mirror over the sink, I was shaking and chewing on my knuckles, I could feel tears wobbling in my eyes, threatening to fall.

'Are you okay?' She laughed through the sentence as she said it, as if she knew it was absurd to ask. She crouched on the floor in front of me and looked up into my face.

'Hey,' she softened slightly. 'Look at me.' I wrenched my gaze from the wall and looked into her eyes. She had a face like Mary Magdalene in a painting. I thought of saints immediately, Joan of Arc's dark hair grazing her cheek. There was a stain of blood under her nose still, I glimpsed a fleck of red on her top lip. Immediately I wondered what it would be like to be her, to walk around the world with a face like that.

'Name five things you can see in the room,' she said, gently but firmly, and I found myself doing it, my pathetic wobbling voice moving haltingly through the items I could see.

'Mirror, towel, bathtub, soap, razor.'

'There we go,' she said, softly, 'now breathe in with me.' She counted to five and I tried to let the air fill my chest but it felt tight, creaky, like it was made of wood.

'Now breathe out with me.' She counted to five again and I deflated. I was almost embarrassed by how quickly the panic left me. I was suddenly aware of how warm I was in my coat, the wet drips of tears and makeup drying on my cheeks. Cautiously she watched me relax.

'I'm Helene,' she said and took my hand, she pulled herself up, then pulled me up with her. 'Take your coat off, you must be too hot.' I wasn't really *too* hot but I did it anyway, I felt I was not supposed to ask her questions. 'Shall we?' she said, motioning towards the door.

'Okay,' I said. 'Sure.'

*

Outside Rosa was standing around looking vaguely irritable.

'Oh my God, there you are,' she said, rolling her eyes exasperatedly. 'How do you know each other?' She gestured to us both, one then the other.

'We just met in the bathroom,' I heard myself say, my body hurt in weird places, my shoulder blade, my chest bone, I already wanted to go home.

Helene said, 'I'm going to get drinks,' she was about to move when Rosa said, 'Helene used to go out with that guy we met at that party, remember?' I felt like I'd missed a step on the stairs. Helene looked hard into my face as the panic passed across it. 'Oh, you know him?' she asked. I wanted to die, I wanted to crawl under the earth, stuff soil in my mouth and suffocate.

'Not really. I mean, yeah a bit I guess.' My eyes slid away from hers but she kept on looking at me, I could feel her gaze flickering against the side of my face. 'I'm going to get us drinks,' she said again and this time she went, I was vaguely aware that Rosa was gossiping about their relation-ship in my ear but I was waiting for Helene to come back, I wanted to keep looking at her, I needed to know her, the need was instant. The plastic cup she handed me had red wine in it, I regarded it warily, back then I didn't really drink red wine.

'Don't worry,' she said, 'it's Malbec, I brought it.' I took a confident sip to show her I trusted her and a blush spread across my cheeks immediately. I became aware that she was also ignoring Rosa and looking only at me. Rosa was telling an elaborate anecdote about the office politics in her publishing job. Helene cut her off mid-sentence.

'And what do you do?' she asked, looking directly at me, I couldn't take it, I fixed my gaze slightly to the right of her head, on an ugly sconce drilled into the wall.

'I'm a waitress in a restaurant in Knightsbridge.' I sort of knew that I needed to have another answer to this ques-tion, some sort of hobby turned career to show that I was not *just* a waitress, that I had other ambitions, but the truth was that somewhere along the line I forgot what it was I was supposed to be doing. I spent my days going to work, sleeping, cooking batches of meals and tidying, then going to work again. Truthfully I had ceased trying to make things better for myself, and I was waiting for something to happen to me instead, I had more or less stopped trying to participate actively in my life.

'Oh, what's it called?'

'Veau.' I tried to explain what street it was on, I was surprised to see recognition cross her face.

'I go there sometimes with my dad.' I pondered the implications of this as Rosa looked for someone else to talk to, she caught the eye of an acquaintance and strode off. I expected Helene to ask if I liked waitressing, whether I had any restaurant-related aspirations, but she didn't and I liked her for this.

'What do you do?' I asked, aware that a silence had fallen between us and that maybe we should be speaking instead of just staring at each other. She took a sip of her wine before she answered, her pauses made my heart thunder, she wasn't afraid that someone was going to interrupt her.

'Right now? I'm an assistant curator in this tiny little gallery. It's mostly just helping super-rich people buy boring art. Mostly I answer the phone, order champagne, you know.' I nodded as if I knew what she was talking about but the truth is this was exactly the kind of job I'd never managed to get, no one ever entrusted me to sit behind a desk, often I had wondered if it had something to do with my weight or my clothes.

'Sometimes I have to go and pick a piece up and bring it to the gallery and that's my whole day. I did it the other day, I took a cab all the way to and from Oxford with this crate of ceramics strapped into the seat next to me.'

'Were they at least really nice ceramics?' I asked, uncertain of what to say, she considered this for a moment.

'I guess?' she shrugged. 'We don't really deal in interesting art, it's just things that people want in their homes.'

'Oh I see.' Of course I understood there was a difference between the sort of art that was good and what rich people actually wanted to own. I'd been in a few of the houses Helene was describing, mostly for my catering job, and I was always shocked by their galling absence of taste, the hulking ugly sofas, the shit black-and-white photography.

'So what happened?' Helene asked flatly.

'What do you mean?'

'Between you and our mutual friend, something happened, didn't it? I can see it on your face.' She took a sip of wine to punctuate the end of her sentence and offered me a tight little smile. Inside I cringed, I could never hide how I was feeling, my expressions were too obvious, everyone could tell what I was thinking. It made me self-conscious, I felt like a child caught doing something wrong by an adult. I bit down on my bottom lip, trying to decide what to tell her. 'I think we have a mutual ex, don't we?' she said, prompting me again.

'I wouldn't call him my ex,' I replied hurriedly, instantly regretting it. It made me sound defensive. I wish I hadn't said anything, I wished I'd never come here, never got dressed, never left the flat, I thought longingly of my tiny flat in the dark.

'Right, right, of course. Well I just wanted to say, woman to woman, he's not a very nice man.' *No shit*, I thought, an intrusive memory of his hand on my face hit me suddenly, the feeling of being pushed down. I shook my head quickly to dislodge it, like a dog trying to clear its ears of water. One side of my face burned like a heat lamp had been turned on it. It was like my whole body was recalling something.

'I kind of figured.'

'Really?' Helene said carefully, her voice was soft and controlled, I could tell she was testing me, gauging my reactions. I felt like a nervous cat quivering under a human's hand.

'We had a sort of violent encounter,' I said before I could stop myself. I hated myself for softening it, for speaking euphemistically when the effects were so concrete. It all seemed connected, like symptoms of the same illness. Something about the profound wrongness of my life had to do with that man and his actions and that evening, I was certain of it.

'Do you mind telling me what happened?' It felt like she had moved even closer, she seemed earnest. My anger moved through me like heat, I was sweating, I wanted to scream, this is not how I envisioned the evening going at all. I tried to choose my words carefully. I took out my phone and found my password-protected photo folder. I typed in the code then passed it across to Helene.

'I was really drunk. Then I woke up like this.' She glanced up at me then down at my phone, a look of disgust on her face. 'You can scroll through,' I said, then I looked down at the floor, it was covered in dust. I took a long sip of wine. I wanted to tell her everything but I didn't know how, I didn't know which word to put in front of the other. I was aware of the shortness of my sentences, the brittle sounds I was making when I tried to talk.

*

Helene finished scrolling then passed the phone back to me, she didn't say anything at first.

'Anyway, I'm sorry,' I said, trying to pre-empt her reaction, 'you said he was your ex. I'm sure you don't want to be reminded of this.' I sounded upset.

'No no!' she said, her voice was high with embarrassment. 'That's not what I meant at all, this is awful, God I'm so so sorry.' She reached across and grabbed my wrist, I didn't move. I knew she was looking at me but I couldn't look back at her because I didn't know what would happen if I did.

'It wasn't like that with us,' she said quietly. 'It was mostly emotional. You know, all that stuff about you can't go here you can't go there. No one likes you, your friends are all terrible, no one will love you like I do. You know, stupid stuff like that. All the clichés. I should have known.'

'That's not stupid at all,' I insisted. 'I'm sorry too.' I moved to take her hand and she took mine, her fingers were cold. I was gazing into her face intensely but her expression was closed. There was a clear furrow in the centre of her forehead, I could feel her rage contained in her small body, even though the tiny furrow was all that was on display. Her face was blank but I could feel her anger like a kind of vibration in her bones.

'Neither of us needs to be sorry,' she said.

'I know, I know. It doesn't feel like that though, does it?' She nodded and let go of my hand.

'Look,' she said, I wasn't crying anymore but she handed me a thick spongy napkin from the table behind her. I got the impression that had we been alone she would have dabbed my face for me.

'We should have coffee,' she said. I didn't know how to respond, if she really wanted to have coffee with me or if this was just something she felt like she had to say. I found the radiating politeness of posh women utterly confusing, I could never tell if it was genuine interest or part of their ongoing collective charm offensive.

'Um. Yeah. That would be nice,' I said.

'Give me your number.' I noticed that Helene's politeness slipped every so often, that she was not used to having to ask for things nicely. She was bossy, a little controlling in her approach. I was surprised she wanted my phone number, even more surprised when she sent me a little tulip emoji so I had her number too. I felt overwhelmed, when Rosa came back I took the opportunity to leave now that Helene would have someone else to talk to.

'Oh okay, well I hope you're okay,' she said briskly, she looked wary and concerned at the same time. 'I'll text you,' she said without looking up at me, and I slipped out without saying anything else to anyone. I had developed a panic about leaving too late at night, it was barely ten thirty and I'd already had enough. The night felt like a total failure, I hadn't spoken to anyone new except for Helene. She was so vivid in my mind that it felt like she was still standing close to me.

*

There is something about residential areas of London that still scares me, even now. When I walked down the street outside the party the sound of my own footsteps was audible, it made me feel like there was something else I should be listening for. I was afraid of my own shadow, convinced that something larger was behind me, in my slipstream. Sometimes I felt like I could hear a second set of footsteps, but when I stopped there was nothing there, just the noise I was making myself. It was always a relief to be back on a crowded train, then on the short walk from the station to my flat. I sent Helene the cherry blossom emoji, hoping she'd respond, but she didn't. I tried to forget about it but she'd made a powerful impression, I felt like I already knew her, she seemed familiar. Even when I was back in my flat I kept seeing her face, I felt crowded by her. I was embarrassed that I'd shown her those photos, that I'd shared something like that with her so quickly. I wondered what she thought of me. I wondered if she looked that good every single day of her life. She had reached out and touched me, she held my elbows in her hands until my body relaxed. I tried to figure how long it had been since someone had touched me affectionately, protectively.

I went through my weird routine three times before I could sleep, checking under the bed which, as always, was too full of suitcases and boxes to conceal a person. I looked behind the curtains and at that little space where the door went when it was open. I pushed the door several times to check it was really locked. I got into bed and shone the little torch light from my phone around the room but there was no one there. Most of the time I didn't even know what I was looking for, the room was too small for me to not notice anyone when I walked in and I didn't know what I would do if I found an intruder. I was afraid of nothing and everything. My sleep had become strange. I slept so deeply that I had trouble getting out of bed in the mornings. My dreams were so frequent and vivid that they might as well have been part of my waking life. In many of them, I was in control, I was the one enacting the violence. The night after the party I was standing in the sports field from my school. The man from the party was smirking at me, it was hard to know why. My anger in the dream was that visceral, hot childhood anger, the anger of the bullied, the humiliated. I punched him in the face, he looked surprised, dazed even.

Blood welled up in his nostrils and I punched him again, he tripped and fell back onto the damp grass, I got on top of him and kept punching. I was still punching when I woke up with a jolt. I was sweating and my knuckles tingled. I thought about my dream, I didn't know what it was like to hit someone like that, I suspected my dream was unrealistic. He was so passive, he didn't even try to fight back. I felt so angry, I burned with rage as I stood in the shower, I burned with rage as I made coffee, I burned with rage as I put on mascara, the face in the mirror was completely tense, I real-ised I'd been grinding my teeth. I hated the people on the trains more than ever. *All of you let this happen*, I thought to myself. *All of you let this happen, I bet none of you would care if I told you about it.*

*

It took days for Helene to reach out. I felt horrible about it, it added a layer of horrible to everything else. I felt guilty about the toxic little crush I was harbouring. I looked at her Instagram on my breaks but it was mainly pictures of paintings in art galleries or trees in parks. I stumbled across a blurry film-camera shot of her face in profile and almost screeched. I was also terrified that she might tell our friends about the pictures in my phone. I knew most of the friends we had in common were under the impression I'd had some kind of one-night stand with the man from the party. I didn't want to shatter that silence and open myself up to pity or worse, questions and doubt. I felt like I'd been bitten by something venomous and if I worked hard enough to keep quiet, my body would just absorb the venom and heal itself. Helene had compromised that scheme and I felt sick over it. I didn't know what she wanted from me. She hadn't checked on me after the panic attack. I wondered how she spent her day, she seemed practical, I imagined her wearing a stylish but rigorously organised backpack to work, putting on reading glasses with tortoiseshell frames.

At work Eva was reading my palm. I was leaning against a wall in the kitchen waiting for dinner service to start. I was trying to think about a party that I had signed up to work at soon but Helene kept barging into my thoughts. *What if she's there?* I thought to myself. *Imagine if she's a customer tonight*, I thought, *while I have to wait on her.* Eva's acrylic nail was digging into my love line.

'You have lots of these,' she said.

'Ouch. What does that mean?'

'It means you're going to have a lot of relationships, lots of instability.'

'Ugh.'

'You're going to get married but you won't know if it's love. You'll have to choose at some point between your marriage and your destiny.' She abruptly turned my palm on its side.

'Jesus, Eva, I thought this was going to be fun.'

'I never said it was going to be fun.' She shrugged, folded my fingers down over my palm and gave me my hand back. She returned to examining her nails, they were bright with green gel, which was technically not allowed but Eva had said that it didn't chip so it was fine.

'And you have a massive crack in your life line, have you ever had a near-death experience?' I pictured car crashes, boating accidents, escaped tigers.

'No. Well, maybe? No,' I said, I thought if I'd really brushed with death, I'd know it somehow, besides I hadn't spoken about the incident with anyone from work, there were too many factors to consider.

'It's a pretty big crack,' she said matter-of-factly, 'you should really be concerned, you could end up totally losing yourself.' Eva was nothing if not confident in her own psychic abilities, we weren't close but I already knew that as a child she banished a ghost from her family home by taking control and telling it to leave. She also claimed to be able to predict the outcome of dice with near-perfect accuracy, the chefs wanted to know why she didn't gamble, Noah, who had been and worked everywhere, kept telling her to go to Vegas.

'Go to Las Vegas, Eva! You could play roulette! Make all your money then come back here and buy me a Tesla.' Veau was riddled with get-rich-quick schemes, petty crime, baggies of cocaine, minor incidents of sexual harassment. When I came back to work after what happened my face was still busted up, even though I took a couple of shifts off, no one asked me about it. Even Noah, who flirted with me shamelessly, only raised his eyebrows and shook his head when he saw me. Noah called me *Princess*. I didn't know if this was supposed to be affectionate or if he'd forgotten my name. Eva lost interest in predicting my future and started folding paper napkins into triangles to go under coffee cups.

'Princess!' Noah yelled at me from across the pass. 'Can you make me a coffee?'

'Yeah sure.' I tried to sound bright, interested, I was just happy to have something to do so I'd look busy, the managers shouted if they caught you standing still. I went through the motions, grinding the beans, tamping the powder into the portafilter, screwing it into the machine, pressing the buttons. Noah used to drink seven or eight espressos a day just to stay awake. I put it on a saucer and passed it over carefully. He paused and picked it up with his whole hand over the rim of the cup. All the chefs picked up the espresso cups like this, I assumed it was so they could avoid touching the tiny handle which would look delicate and feminine.

'You're getting better at these,' he said. It was almost a compliment.

'Thanks.' I looked away, casting for something else to do so no one would berate me for leaning against the back wall.

'Have you eaten yet?' he asked.

'No.'

'Here.' He chucked various sides onto a dinner plate for me, this was how the chefs used to feed me when they remembered, because they knew I wouldn't eat meat and the vegetarian alternatives were too few and precious to give out to staff. He spooned something out of a small pan into a ramekin and nestled it in the centre of the plate.

'What's that?' I asked, pointing at it.

'I want you to try it,' he said and took another sip of his coffee.

'Yes, but what is it?'

'It's mussels! Shellfish! Okay?'

'No, I don't eat that. Take them back.' I didn't know then why he was like this with me, Eva hardly ever ate the restaurant food, she claimed to be watching her weight, the only thing I ever saw her eat was one of the stale dinner rolls – I can see her now, backed up against a wall, chewing on it. My vegetarianism was a big joke to the chefs, they thought it was hilarious to have principles when it came to food.

'Why, because they're so cute? You don't want to hurt them?' Noah asked me. This was a recurring theme, the chefs were always showing me cow's heads, pig trotters, asking if I was going to cry.

'Princess, they are basically bugs. They don't have any thoughts. I cooked them all nice with white wine, cream, shallot, fucking dill, just try one.' I realised there was no way out of the interaction without either eating a mussel or causing offence, so I chose to eat the mussel rather than screw up my own chances of getting fed further down the line. I picked one up, dug its rubbery interior out with a fork and chewed. I expected it to be fishy and it was, but mainly I tasted sea water. It tasted of shallot, cream and white wine.

'Thank you, Noah,' I said after a moment.

'You're welcome. Jesus. Now eat quickly, it's all about to kick off.' He was right, I looked at the clock, ten to six. I turned away from the pass so he wouldn't watch me eat and shovelled creamed spinach, honeyed carrots, potatoes, a second kind of potato into my mouth as fast as I could. I felt like I stayed fuller for longer when I ate everything fast. I even ate all of the little mussels, apologising to them internally as I chewed, then I drank the cream sauce out of the ramekin. *I bet you do have thoughts*, I thought as I ate. *I'm sorry I ate you and your thoughts.* I thought about the mussels the whole evening, it helped me to stay calm, imagining them growing underwater, peacefully slurping up any speck that floated past. I went home that night and fell asleep in front of a documentary about manta rays. They moved slowly and hugely across my screen until I passed out in front of it. I had the volume on the manta ray documentary turned up so high I could barely hear the people talking in the corridor, right outside my door. The stairs in my building were uneven, anyone going up or

31

down those stairs announced themselves in the sound of creaking floorboards. I used to hear those creaking sounds again and again throughout the night. It used to wake me up from my fitful post-shift sleep. I thought maybe someone in the flats upstairs was having a gathering, it would explain the hushed voices and the footsteps running up and down the creaking stairs. At some point during the night these noises were replaced by a different sound, it was like someone was slowly, laboriously moving a piece of furniture across the landing. The sound was grating, *drag drag* it went, on and on, *drag drag*. I finally hauled myself out of bed and into the twilight of my room, the streetlights outside meant the flat was never completely dark, it was permanently in a kind of greyscale. I pressed my ear against the door and I could hear it still, that sound of something heavy being shifted. I unlocked my door and peered out onto the landing, there was no one there, nothing moving, outside my bedsit it was completely silent and dark.

*

I lived alone, the bedsit was too small to accommodate any-one else, often it felt too small to accommodate me. The size of the flat meant I slept in my kitchen. There were two large windows on one side of the flat and I slept on the other side. In one quick sweep I could see everything I owned, except for the clothes and shoes I kept under the bed. It was cheap, but I shared the bathroom with the other people who lived on the floor. If I wasn't careful I could miss my opportunity to shower in the morning. I used to like my own company but increasingly I found myself spending *all* my time on my own. I used to fantasise about living with someone I loved, this person was always shadowy, their functions mainly domestic. I wanted someone else to clean up after dinner, take my dirty clothes to the laundrette when I didn't feel like it. I needed the feeling of someone else nearby, their energy, their chatter. I stopped being able to sleep without some kind of white noise to distract me. I always had to have something playing in the background: a sitcom, a cartoon, a YouTube tutorial about how to make beignets. I found it unbearable to sit in silence. It made me anxious, twitchy. I didn't like anything intense, emotional or violent. I found it hard to watch anything that wasn't a nineties sitcom. I watched them illegally on a site full of pop-ups for hot sex with singles in my area, bitcoin investments, VPN etc. I liked the colour palettes of these old sitcoms, they looked soft and muted. People on them told jokes about first dates, office politics. Nothing truly bad ever happened in their worlds, and if it did, it was over quickly. It felt like all the new TV shows my friends were watching were full of rape scenes. I wondered if it had always been like this and I just hadn't noticed before. I ruled out detective dramas, critically acclaimed period pieces, edgy sarcastic comedy dramas with interesting female leads were out of the question. It wasn't worth it. I figured what was the point of trying to watch something zeitgeisty if I was just going to end up pausing it to have another panic attack, sit with my head between my knees. It felt unfair.

*

Of course I went looking for answers on the internet. There were forums, like there were for every aspect of the human experience. The women on the forums insisted on

33

calling themselves *survivors* but it didn't feel right for me. I didn't want to call myself a *victim* either, like a different, smaller percentage of the women. I could only imagine it like this: it was like I had been in the path of a natural disaster. Like there was a landslide and I was looking the other way, doing some other kind of activity, washing the dishes, looking out of a window that faced away from the mountain, and then I was crushed to death, buried under rubble and debris. I just wasn't paying attention. Lots of the people on the forums seemed to think I should've gone to the police in the twenty-four hours after, let them ask questions, take swabs. I knew I didn't have the strength, I wondered what kind of person would. Besides, I knew there were too many grey areas, too much alcohol involved, too many of our mutual friends. I knew it would involve recounting the story over and over, getting my facts straight. It felt insurmountable. I had done one thing right, I still had the pictures of my body from the morning. I didn't quite know why I'd taken them, maybe I thought it would wake me up, like when you search for electronics in a dream. It didn't work but at least I had some evidence in a password-protected folder, Helene was the only one who'd seen them.

God, Helene. I was obsessed with her instantly, I thought about her all the time. The second I let my mind wander there she was, idling in a doorway, looking arrogantly back at me. I could see her face so clearly in my imagination. She was there all through my shifts as I went through all my regular motions, polishing cutlery, clearing plates. I looked at her Instagram when I locked myself in the restaurant bathroom. I scrolled through further and further until I saw a picture she'd taken of herself. It was a mirror selfie, part of her face artfully obscured, I breathed in sharply looking at the way her dark hair fell against her cheek.

*

Days passed and I kept waking up with the sensation of something heavy sitting on my chest. I struggled to take deep breaths in the mornings. Sometimes I would wake up drenched in sweat, my hair plastered to my forehead, other times I'd wake up icy cold, shivering violently, pulling my duvet around myself in a tight cocoon. Everything seemed like it was tinged with grey. I made pasta sauce, fried tofu, it all tasted the same to me. I downloaded a dating app and swiped yes to some strangers' faces. I ignored them when they tried to talk to me, I went to bed as early as I could, I had nothing to look forward to.

*

When Helene finally sent me a text I slept through it. I had silenced all my devices because everything was making me jittery, the little chirps of the notifications were suddenly too much for me to bear. I looked at my phone as soon as I woke up, the first thing my eyes focused on in the morning was that screen. There usually wasn't much to look at, some news notifications telling me about fires, outbreaks of disease, politicians and their sex scandals, a series of white bricks from the strangers on the app. None of their messages made me feel anything and then I saw **Hello, coffee on Tuesday afternoon?** The tone was odd, it made me feel like we had already made the plan and she was only confirming it. I looked at her name on the screen, *Helene*.

My brain wasn't entirely awake, I replied as fast as I could **Yes! Where? What time?** I watched it deliver, slowly I realised how pathetically eager I seemed, it got worse and worse as I looked at it. I rested the phone screen down on my head, the sweat from my forehead sticking it in place. I noticed the screen lighting up from its position on my head.

Nordic Bakery, 5pm?

Sounds good! I replied immediately, adding the little tea-cup emoji. She saw the message but didn't reply. Going to work felt like a ridiculous task, I wanted to stay perfectly still until it was time to get ready to go and see Helene. It sounded like my neighbours were moving things outside my door again, I heard scraping, footsteps again, up and down then up and down the stairs. I pulled the duvet over my head, *Please don't knock on my door*, I thought, *please don't knock on my door*. The third time I thought the sentence, hard in my mind, the noise stopped.

*

The kitchen was always hotter than I remembered, there was no configuration of the uniform that would have made it comfortable to work there. It was like a sauna, like I was being cooked alive in the oil and steam. I always smelled of sweat and animal fat. I pushed my hair up on top of my head and tried to secure it in a bun, away from my neck. Noah pushed a plate loaded with food at me and I took my hands out of my hair to catch it before it slid off the pass.

'What is this?' I asked him, I didn't recognise the food from the menu. He pointed to the different items on the plate forcefully.

'Potato rosti, salmon, sour cream.' I wanted to tell him I was trying not to eat fish anymore but I was so hungry and wanted to sit somewhere quiet, away from the noise and the heat in the kitchen.

'Thank you. That's really kind, thank you,' I said awkwardly and he nodded back without making eye contact with me. I went out of the kitchen and tried to find somewhere to sit, both dining rooms were already laid up for dinner so I shut myself in the storeroom. It was quiet there, among the stacks of table linen. I knew I would be in trouble if anyone found me there with food so I tried to be quick. I sat down on a kick stool, I'd forgotten to bring cutlery so I picked up the potato rosti with my hands. They were golden and crispy, I could see the little grains of salt on the surface. I picked up a blanket of salmon, covered the rosti in it and tried to use this construction to scoop up sour cream. It was the most delicious thing I'd eaten for weeks. The rostis were too hot to hold in my hand comfortably but I didn't care. With no one watching I ate rapidly and indulgently, I sucked the fat and salt from my fingers. Too soon, my plate was empty and I headed back to the kitchen, sneaking my plate onto a stack of dirty ones near the pot-washing station. When I went back to the pass all the chefs were busy in the run-up to service.

'Noah?' I said to his back, hoping he wouldn't hear me. He turned around, grinning.

'Look at this, Princess.' He was moving a teaspoon through a thick substance in a cloudy plastic tub, it was gold and glossy, I remember I liked the colour.

'What is it?'

'Schmaltz.' My brain shuffled through the different meanings, sentimental nonsense, romantic things. 'It's chicken fat,' he said, smiling hugely at me.

'Ugh, why would you show me that?' I said, suddenly disgusted.

'It's what I cooked the latkes in.' He laughed a quick hooting laugh at me. My stomach sank, I felt sick again, and furious, I wondered if I was going to throw up. *There's chicken fat churning through me*, I thought, *bird fat, fat made from birds.* I went totally silent.

'What do you think about that, Princess? It tasted good, right?' My face grew hot.

'Why would you do that?' I said, my voice louder than usual. 'What was the point of that?' I said, even louder. Noah's mouth dropped open. I panicked and walked out of the kitchen. He shouted after me.

'It tastes better! I made them for you!' I was so angry over this weird little betrayal but I knew in the back of my mind that shouting at Noah was upsetting the food chain. The chefs decided when and what we ate. If Noah thought I was stuck up maybe I would never get to eat anything at work ever again. Our coats and bags were stored on hooks in a corridor adjacent to the kitchen, we couldn't even hide things in there to eat on the sly.

There wasn't anything for me to do in the dining rooms, the tables were all laid, the candles all lit. I stood there for a second enjoying the quiet, the smell of burning wax reminded me of Christmas. I breathed in and out slowly, then I turned around and went back to the kitchen. I took down a spray bottle and dish cloth from the shelf and started to wipe down the surfaces. I still needed to look occupied.

'Hey Princess!' Noah yelled from over the pass.

'Yeah?' I shouted back without turning around, there was a pause.

'I'm sorry.' His voice was quieter now, I could hear that he was standing close behind me, I turned around.

'It's okay,' I said. I folded the dish cloth and started making stacks of cups and saucers for easy access on top of the coffee machine.

'But it was good though, right?' he asked, twisting a cloth napkin in his hands. All the chefs were the same, frustrated artists, their hours were worse than mine, they badly wanted compliments, even from me, they always needed praise and they hardly ever got it.

'Yes, it was excellent,' I replied, honestly. After I'd said this he started to look bashful, I added sarcastically, laying it on thick, 'You're a very talented chef.' Noah clutched at his chest theatrically.

'Oh you break my heart, Princess!' He grinned as he went back to rapidly stirring cream into a dark brown sauce, I watched it change colour until someone shouted at me to move.

*

The shift passed in a violent blur. I walked as fast and carefully as I could to the dining room and back to the kitchen, I don't know how many times. I said as little as I could get away with. Ten p.m. rolled around and I started to flag. I distractedly grasped the espresso maker's red-hot steamer wand with my bare hand and had to stand with my fingers under the cold stream of water in the hand-washing sink for ten minutes while I waited for it to stop burning. I hated it, the pain was immense and I didn't like to think of my hand in the sink, quietly searing like a steak every time I turned off the tap to check on it. I watched all the other waiters dart back and forth like fish in an aquarium, trying to calculate what time it would be when I got home, until I suddenly realised: it was less than a day until I was going to see Helene.

*

I didn't know what to wear. Everything was wrong for the occasion, too dressy, too short, didn't fit me anymore, couldn't stretch over my thighs. Everything had a hole in it or was covered in tiny bobbles from having been washed too many times. When I pictured Helene her clothes were always simple, black cigarette trousers and a grey cashmere turtleneck, a black silk shift dress. I imagined small touches of jewellery, thin gold pins threaded through her ears, a single hammered silver ring. I could never wear anything like that, office wear made me look frumpy. A shift dress was out of the question, my thighs and chest were too large, ungainly for something like that. I had to try harder than someone like Helene to look smart, I had to look more feminine, keep my hair longer, and put on lipstick. Helene didn't have to wear makeup because she got her eyebrows threaded and went to see an expensive dermatologist. I could tell. If she ever bothered to wear lipstick she would look utterly devastating. Just picturing it made me want to close my eyes. I settled on something girly, predictable. I put on tights, a long shiny skirt, a pink sweatshirt and a boyish long coat. I wore the coat a lot, it looked expensive because it fit me well but it was made of thin polyester and it was no use in the cold at all.

*

I thought I was too early to the cafe, I paced back and forth in front of it for a few minutes, wondering what I should do. I paused to peer inside, make an assessment, and there was Helene. Her head bent slightly over a book, her left hand moving over her right arm, pushing up her sleeve so she could look at her watch. I breathed out hard and pushed open the door, watching her the whole time. She didn't look up even though the door had a bell attached. I walked all the way over to her table and stood in front of her before she noticed me.

'Hey it's you,' she said, giving me a small smile. She didn't get up.

'That's me!' I said, not knowing exactly what I was trying to say. 'Do you need anything?' I asked, waving my debit card vaguely at the table.

'No, that's okay, I'm all right.' She picked up her teacup to show me, she was drinking herbal tea out of one of those squat little teapots.

'Oh okay, I'm just going to get a coffee.' I threw an arm back to show I meant I was going to go to the till.

'No, no,' she said, 'let me.' She raised her hand and a waiter appeared out of nowhere, glancing nervously between the two of us, holding a pad and pencil.

'What would you like?' she said, like she owned the place.

'A filter coffee?' I said, panicking, I watched the waiter as he began scribbling, and then craned my neck to look back at the food on display by the till. 'And a cookie?' I said, the waiter looked petrified.

'What kind of cookie?' he asked, his eyes darting between the two of us again.

'How many different kinds do you have?' Helene asked.

41

'There's milk chocolate, white chocolate and macadamia nut, double chocolate, dark chocolate and ginger, um, there's one more—'

'That one!' I said, hoping to spare him from trying to remember the rest of the list. 'Dark chocolate and ginger sounds great.' It did sound great, I hadn't found a good time to eat that day and all of a sudden I was starving. The waiter scuttled off, I pulled the chair out from behind the table and sat down, shrugging my coat off until it pooled behind me on the seat. Helene put a tassel bookmark in her book and was pouring herself another cup of tea, the colour was murky and greenish and the smell made my head swim.

'That was the cookie I was going to suggest,' she said.

'Oh really?' I asked, delighted.

'Yes, I come here all the time and that seemed like the right cookie for you.' I couldn't tell if she was making fun of me or not. The truth was that if I'd been alone I might have gone for the double chocolate but I didn't want her to think my figure was because of all my double-chocolate cookie choices. I didn't know what to say to her.

'Were you at work today?' I asked.

'Yeah I was sitting at the front desk. The smasher came back,' she said, as if this was a perfectly normal thing to say.

'The smasher?'

'Oh have I not told you about the smasher?' She took a long sip of her tea, she was always taking these long pauses in the middle of conversation. 'We have these little ceramics for sale in front of the till, they're pretty expensive. We sell them but we just take cash into this little lock box, anyway. Sometimes people want to return them because their friend already has a similar one or something.'

42

'Sure,' I said, trying to imagine myself buying, or for that matter returning, an expensive miniature ceramic.

'Anyway this one lady has realised that when people return them, because they're pretty unique, even if they don't have a receipt we just give them the cash back. So she's started picking up one of these little things at a time, pretending to have a look and then she turns away and dashes them against the shelf when she thinks I'm not looking, then she tries to return the thing for cash.'

'Oh my God.' I was laughing pretty hard imagining what kind of person would try and carry off this grift. 'Does that ever work?'

'No!' Helene said. She looked outraged at the suggestion. 'You can hear it when someone breaks a piece like that.' The waiter returned with my coffee and cookie. He looked at Helene as he set them down.

'Thanks,' I said but he wasn't looking at me. Helene nodded at him and continued talking.

'That's the crazy thing, I don't think we've ever given her any money, she just keeps coming back and breaking things.' I was growing to admire the smasher, her scam, the confidence to keep coming back to a high-end gallery and try to rip them off by destroying their merchandise, it didn't seem any morally worse to me than my waitering jobs.

'That's incredible,' I said and looked down at my cookie. It was enormous, practically the size of the plate it was sitting on, I broke it into several shards and began to eat it.

'Well, you must get a lot of characters in the restaurant,' Helene said, waving a hand dismissively. I considered this for a moment.

43

'I definitely meet more weird people when I'm doing catering gigs. Because it's often for people's family events, or weddings.'

'Ooh, tell me more.' She sat forward a little, I accidentally looked right into the centre of her eyes. I hastily looked down.

'Well they get these ridiculous party planner people in to make everything the same sort of aesthetic, you know? So I inevitably end up serving people drinks out of a test tube, or a hamper or something large, heavy and slippery.' It was not as fun a story as I might have hoped. 'There was that party where I was hit on by a Frank Sinatra impersonator.'

'Amazing!' she said, and it had been pretty funny, he was serenading me too aggressively and I tripped trying to avoid him and threw crab salad all over an important man's expensive shoes. I didn't know how to convey this to Helene, I just kept looking at her and she kept looking at me. It was like we already knew each other. We weren't talking about anything personal because we didn't need to. I felt a creeping sense of doom, something like guilt and fear. Looking at her felt like staring down a well, I kept hoping I'd see the bottom, something to rest my eyes on, but there was just darkness and more darkness. She was the first one to break the stare.

'Do you mind if you get one thing straight first?' The doom expanded in my chest, I had looked down the well and now I was falling into it.

'Yes of course.'

'When I first met you I liked you *immediately*,' she said forcefully, she looked me squarely in the face, I struggled to keep looking into her eyes, I tried to look at the middle of her forehead. 'I knew then we were going to be close and I'm never wrong about these things.'

I laughed nervously. 'I liked you too.' She gave me a little smile. 'How's my face?' I asked, moving it from side to side for her to check for crumbs. She reached out and held my chin for a second, examining me in profile.

'Perfect. Now, if you want to speed up and eat the rest of your cookie, I suggest we go and get a *real* drink, what do you think?' I knew it wasn't really a question but I wanted to agree with her anyway.

'Yes. That sounds perfect.'

*

I tried to get her to help me eat the cookie but she would only accept a small fragment, leaving me to scarf the whole thing. She didn't go up to the counter to pay, preferring to theatrically leave a £20 note on the table and leave without waiting for her change. When we walked down the street she didn't wait to reach the crossing, she pulled me into the street behind her, striding impatiently through the honking traffic, holding up her arm. She was wearing a little chiffon scarf that trailed out behind her in the breeze. I remember thinking it was the kind of accessory I could never pull off, it'd look fussy on me but on her it looked unstudied, chic even. I was a little relieved when I realised the pub she'd chosen was the same as every other pub I'd been to in London. She drank straight whisky.

'God,' I remember saying in hushed tones after she'd ordered, 'could you try to be a little bit less cool please, people are going to wonder what you're doing here with me.' I was surprised when she blushed a little, blotches appeared on her face and neck.

45

'Oh I'm sure they can figure it out.' She raised an eyebrow and I looked away again.

*

She paid for several rounds, each time pushing my card away, pulling a face as if I was being ridiculous. I found myself laughing harder, smiling more, touching her arm. I listened to her talk at length about her education, her job. By our third drink she fixed me with her eyes again and grabbed the lapel of my coat firmly, feeling the material with her fingers. I choked a little on my gin and tonic.

'What are you doing?' I asked, trying not to cough.

'The coat, I like it, it gives you a sort of masculine energy.'

'People are always saying that I have that and I have no idea what it means,' I said, unsure if I should be insulted.

'It means you're sexy.'

'You think I'm sexy?'

'Not necessarily, I'm saying it's an empirical fact that you are sexy.' She refused to give anything away, I broke down laughing, she looked very serious.

'Your laugh!' she said. 'It's so much louder than your regular speaking voice.'

'Oh God it is, isn't it?' I said self-consciously, it had been a long time since I'd really laughed. 'Hey, stop observing me.' Helene released my coat and downed the rest of her whisky without responding. 'Time to go,' she said and pulled me up by grabbing both of my arms. 'I don't live far from here, you can stay with me, I don't want you going home in the dark.'

*

Everything in her flat was beautiful and tasteful. She had a blue velvet sofa, it was so thick and soft I felt like I was lying across the back of a bear. I ran a hand over it and it changed colour under my fingers. I felt warm and a bit dizzy. When I tried to sit up I saw Helene was standing over me, pouring another cloudy cocktail out of a metal cocktail shaker. She handed me the glass, it was a coupe with little stars chipped into it. I suspected it was vintage, or maybe something she inherited, a nice housewarming gift from a family member. I worried I was going to drop it.

'You know, ever since we met that night, I feel very protective over you.' She sat down in the adjacent armchair, then shifted around so her legs dangled off the arm. She jiggled her legs until one of her shoes fell off, she kicked her other leg and the shoe flew off and smacked against something on the other side of the room.

'Oh yeah?' I said, unsure of whether she needed me to respond.

'Yes. I mean, he did this to both of us, didn't he?'

'Sure,' I said.

Helene took a deep breath and rested her manicured hand over her eyes. Her face was flushed, she had been touching her hair and it was parted on the wrong side.

'You know my grandmother used to tell me stories about the woods. They were so terrifying. Girls were always disappearing. There was one in particular, I remember, about a girl who climbed up a tree in front of her mother and just never came down again. Do you ever wonder what actually happened to those girls? I just assumed a man kidnapped her, maybe even killed her, that it was a euphemism, that thing about being taken away by the faeries. What she really meant was if you meet a stranger in the woods you'll never come out again.' She was talking faster than usual, I wondered if she was as drunk as I was. I thought about the sounds outside the flat. I thought about telling her about them. I opened my mouth to tell her but she was still speaking.

'You know what I think?' I shook my head. 'I think we should kill him.' She looked into my eyes as she took a long sip. I laughed hard and humourlessly, raised my eyebrows.

'Yeah, maybe,' I said. 'That seems like the only option, doesn't it?' Helene didn't say anything, she just eyed me watchfully like a cat.

'Why not?' she said finally. 'The state can't manage the problem of violence against women or other marginalised people for that matter.' She stumbled a little over the syllables, I tried not to laugh. 'In fact it keeps *doing* the violence. Maybe it's up to us to fix the problem.'

'And how are we going to *fix* this *problem?*' I asked, I thought it was a philosophical question, that she was being facetious. But there was something tempting about it at the same time, not the physical act but the prospect of a world without the man from the party in it, even the thought of it made me feel more relaxed. Helene took a gulp of her drink and stared off into space.

'I told you,' she said, 'he needs to die.'

'Okay, well, keep me updated on your plan for that.' I was still lying down on the couch. Helene put her drink down on a side table then she stood up, bent down and took mine out of my hand. I let her, she leaned over and grazed her thumb against my bottom lip. She kissed me and her mouth was warm and soft, I leaned into it, my hand moving against her face, it felt impossibly small and delicate like the bone of her jaw was just barely covered by her skin.

When she pulled away I was a little disappointed, frightened I had done something wrong.

'I'm going to bed,' she said, standing up. 'You can come with me if you want.' I didn't hesitate, I followed her.

*

'Your bed is enormous,' I said to Helene when she came back from the bathroom, she was rubbing her eyes with her knuckles. 'How do you decide where to sleep?' She snorted and climbed into the other side.

'Yes, maybe it seems silly but I love it, I don't think I could sleep in a regular bed anymore.' I considered my own double bed, how it would be dwarfed next to this thing. The bed seemed giant and stark like Helene and I were lying on opposite sides of an ice floe. I wondered how you would go about getting close to someone in a bed like this. It seemed profoundly unromantic, to sleep next to someone in a bed where they could slip out and you might not even notice.

'I had a girlfriend at university,' I heard myself saying, 'we always used to stay in my single bed so, when we went away for the weekend we were in a double bed and she was like where are you? I can't find you!' I laughed nervously at the end of this anecdote, feeling a little on edge. It was true, I used to sleep completely tangled up with her, once or twice I fell asleep face down on her chest. I used to fall asleep easily.

Helene was lying in bed, looking up at me. She had propped herself up on her elbow, her fingertips buried in her hair. She was wearing matching navy silk pyjamas. I coveted them immediately. She was half listening, half waiting for her turn to speak.

49

'Have you dated a lot of women?' she asked, I felt myself tense up.

'Not really, I haven't dated a lot of anyone.' I paused, chewing on my lip self-consciously. My connections with other people tended to be fleeting, they always fell apart in a matter of months.

'Me neither,' she said.

'Really?' I asked, I sounded hopeful.

'Yes. I don't really like . . . anyone, really,' she said, I could feel her watching me but I was afraid to return the look. I thought it could hurt me somehow, like staring into a bright light. She said my name and I realised her hand was on top of my wrist, her thumb was rubbing against its soft underside. I felt very vulnerable, like a sea creature pulled out of water. She pulled me further down into the bed with her, snaked her arm around my waist and kissed my neck. I was completely aware of the ways she was moving my body, how I was supposed to arrange it for her.

*

The next morning I collected my things as quietly as I could, I got out of the flat without even checking to see if she was awake. I was seized with panic from the moment I woke up, I didn't know what I was doing, in this neighbourhood, with this woman. Her place and the houses around hers were all beautiful, black painted doors, white columns, brass doorbells, roses in the front gardens. I was desperate to get home, be alone with my thoughts. My brain felt like it was full of jangling bells. When I checked my phone it was still painfully early, I figured I could get home and sleep for a few hours before my shift. I was rushing towards the station when I felt nausea building in my stomach. I stopped dead, took a deep breath and puked right into someone's manicured flower patch. I lurched back up and ran the rest of the way to the station.

In my flat the light wouldn't turn on. I switched it angrily back and forth then gave up. I locked the door, threw my coat on the floor and climbed into my own bed. My sheets felt so much worse than Helene's had. *I can never bring her here*, I thought miserably. I looked at the time and did a mental calculation. I could sleep for two hours before I had to get ready and go to work at the catering event. I checked my emails for details of the shift. My heart sank, they were bussing us out to the suburbs, it was someone's family thing. A 50th Birthday Party. For some godforsaken reason it was *The Great Gatsby* themed. *God, I hope I'm the one who dies in the pool*, I thought. They wanted us to wear black shirts and trousers, my white shirt wasn't clean anyway so that was okay with me. I put on a rain sounds podcast and fell asleep immediately. My sleep was fitful. I kept falling into this half sleep where there was a figure standing by my door, half hidden in the twilight of sleep. I started awake and blinked until I could recognise there wasn't anything there. I fell asleep again and the figure moved to the side of my bed, the dripping sounds of the white noise rain podcast mixed with the figure and the figure dripped dark water into my carpet. I sat up hard and rubbed my eyes and it disappeared. I made a mental note to google sleep paralysis/alcohol, and got out of bed.

*

On the way to the shift I bought one of my safety meals. A paper bag of supermarket doughnuts. They were only a pound and they filled up my stomach. All I had at home was some cheap spaghetti and the can of Heinz tomato soup I kept around in case I got ill. When I got stressed or tired my eating was the first thing to go wrong. I went through these phases where everything I usually ate seemed repulsive and strange. Eggs especially had the capacity to inspire terror, when I didn't feel good, the thought of an undercooked egg made my stomach turn over. When I got like that I had to eat something unhealthy and bland, plain Pringles, garlic bread, chips with salt but not vinegar. I had to wait for that feeling to pass. It didn't matter how hungry I was, the aversions made choosing a meal impossible. When they ruined the possibility of eating the food in the restaurant I told the chefs I was ill, then gnawed on a dry bread roll in the walk-in freezer.

*

No one on the minibus to the event seemed to want to talk, it was painfully quiet, we all stared balefully out of the window in our matching shirts and trousers. The doughnuts slightly dampened my hangover but my feelings of shame and panic still prowled around my stomach. I had my head leaned against the window and my phone wedged between my thighs when I noticed it light up with a message from Helene. I looked down at it. **My neighbours say someone puked on their roses, you wouldn't know anything about that would you?** Then she had typed several of the crazy person emojis, the winking face with its tongue out. I felt irritable, I felt like replying, *maybe I wouldn't have puked* *in their roses if you hadn't gotten me drunk.* Internally I tried to rephrase it but any way I wanted to put it sounded a little petty and resentful. I was remembering why I tried not to drink the night before a shift. I swiped and made Helene's message disappear. I didn't know how to talk to her. The bus pulled into the driveway of a beautiful Regency-era house, I instantly wondered what it would be like to live there.

'All right!' my supervisor yelled as he ripped open the side doors of the minibus, he was a short man wearing a three-piece polyester suit. 'Let's do it!'

*

At first it felt like any other shift. The catering chefs were a lot quieter than the chefs I was used to, they didn't yell at each other, they gave me a blue plastic icing bag and they let me pipe little peaks of mascarpone into fruit tarts. I much preferred this sort of task to waitering, I liked the careful precise work, making a row of canapés look identical. I liked it so much more than chatting with customers, it was less psychologically demanding than having to schmooze, laugh at their jokes. The living room in the centre of the house was so vast that a band set up a little performance area at the edge of a temporary dance floor. I tried to remember how to box a tablecloth for the bar they were setting up, but eventually another girl came along and did it for me. There was an inexplicable gender divide on these shifts where the men on the shift always ran the bar and the women always held the trays of food. I didn't get it but I didn't question it either. I was told to circulate with my tray of mini quiches, smile. I was doing what I always did, walking around, hovering near clumps of people who were arriving and milling about with their full glasses of champagne. My tray was only half empty when I saw him. He was wearing a blue shirt and jeans, he was underdressed, at ease with the people around him, he was laughing, gesturing with his half-full glass. I could see him but he hadn't yet noticed me. I couldn't move from where I was standing, I was rigid like a wild animal facing an oncoming car. I watched in slow horror as his eyes moved across the room to me and his face changed to a look of recognition. I had assumed, on some level, that the anonymity of the job would protect me, that there was no way anyone from my life could recognise me in my catering disguise. But there he was, walking towards me.

'Hello!' he said, jovial, a little shy. *I could hit him*, I thought, *I could throw the rest of the quiches on the ground and beat him with this metal tray.*

'Hi,' I said.

'You look so freaked out,' he said confidently, I imagined him with a broken nose, blood dripping onto his periwinkle shirt.

'I never see anyone from my real life at my job,' I said, this was true, at least.

'Oh, that's funny.' He sipped from the champagne flute and looked into my eyes, his eyes had no depth to them at all, they were flat like the eyes of a shark. 'Listen, I've been thinking we should have a conversation at some point.' *Oh God*, I thought, *why?*

'Oh really?' I remember my voice was light and totally foreign to me, like a recording was playing. Inside my head I carefully repeated *I am at work I am at work I am at work* to myself.

'Yeah! I think it would be nice to sort of clear the air, y'know? We're in a lot of the same circles, we were bound to run into each other.'

'I should really get back to work,' I said, desperate to exit the conversation. *Maybe I could hide in the kitchen*, I thought, *maybe I could run away into the night.*

'Sure sure, yes of course, well, I'll message you?' He reached out and put his hand on my shoulder. *This isn't really happening*, I thought to myself, *I'm not really here.*

'Great. Sounds good!' I heard the words come out of my mouth, I hated the friendly way I had spoken, it was so deeply at odds with how I felt that the words clanged dissonantly in my head. I wanted to rip the skin off my shoulder. I walked quickly back into the kitchen and put down the tray.

'You don't look so good,' my supervisor said. He was smirking a little, eating one of the canapés. There was a blue plastic tub under the table that was supposed to be for the dregs of champagne from the empty flutes. I contemplated it for a second, then pulled it out and puked into it. I couldn't stop hurling bile and chewed-up dough, the sickness went through my body in waves like the movement of a snake. The noises over my head went from angry and disgusted to genuinely concerned. When I looked up I was sweating, and there was a cluster of men looking down at me.

'You know you really shouldn't come to work if you're not well,' my supervisor said. There was a whole procedure for getting signed off a shift once you'd agreed to it, it involved getting a doctor's note.

'I didn't know I was ill,' I said groggily. 'It just *happened*.'

'Christ,' he said, 'it could be a stomach bug. We can't let the client see this. Give me that.' He took the plastic tub off me. 'Max will drive you back to the station.' The man I assumed was Max looked uncertain and a little frightened.

'I'm sorry, I'm really sorry,' I said mechanically.

'Whatever. It's fine,' my supervisor said, it was clear he just wanted me out, he didn't want to have to look at me anymore. I felt dreadful as I gathered my things, sweaty and feverish, then cold and shivering. I wondered vaguely if this was my body's way of getting me out of the situation. I wondered what zone we were in. Max said nothing on the drive, he was worried I'd throw up on the minibus and kept glancing at me furtively. I thanked him when I got off at the station and he grunted. The station was totally quiet, my nausea passed as I waited for the train with my head bent over my lap. My whole body felt numb, I didn't feel anything anymore.

*

I got an email asking passive-aggressively if I was *feeling better* and if so whether I could be a reserve for an event tonight. I put on the same clothes I'd worn the day before and trekked all the way across London. When I arrived, I hardly knew how I'd got there. The hour-long journey had both taken forever and slipped by, like a journey in a dream. The woman in charge of the event counted my head among the heads who had already arrived, then told me they had enough staff and that I should go home. I did the maths, deducting my travel costs, I'd made around £20 that whole day. In the underground there were adverts for a horror film where a faceless woman was wearing a bloodstained white slip. I scowled at the poster whenever I saw it. I got on a train and tried not to look at anyone else on it. I pulled my scarf up over the bottom of my face.

*

It was starting to feel like the theme of the year was violence. Every site I scrolled through it was violence and more violence. They called it harassment or terrorism or whatever but that's what it was, violence. Celebrities kept talking about it. Everywhere, the women were talking, the women were being heard, the men too were talking, all anybody did was *talk* about it. I was supposed to be glad that everyone was finally talking about it, I was supposed to be grateful for the *conversation*. I didn't want to talk about it anymore. I wanted it all to go away. I thought about getting a baseball bat and storing it under my bed. I watched internet videos about how to free your wrists from zip-ties. I read a wikiHow article about how to kick out the tail lights of a car from inside the boot. The idea is that you rip up the inside lining of the car and put your foot through the plastic eye of the light. Then you can stick your arm out and wave it, attracting the attention of passers-by. I wondered if anyone had done this before, if it was proven to work. I kept thinking about the gulf between reading about it on my laptop and being in the boot of a car. Images came to me, unbidden, at inappropriate moments. Moments when I wanted stillness and quiet, the undercurrent of violence had broken through to the surface, I had been knocked over by the tide. My own memories joined the assault; getting shoved to the ground, too drunk to get up. Some were so horrible they seemed unlikely, like how could I have hidden this from

57

myself for so long? It wasn't that bad, was it? It couldn't possibly have been that bad.

*

Everything got really weird. Things in my flat kept breaking. A second bulb in the centre of the ceiling glowed much too bright then blew dramatically, plunging me into darkness. I couldn't be bothered to buy another one so I used my lamp and existed in the soupy semi-dark. My crockery seemingly couldn't stay in my hands, a piece seemed to fall off the side in the kitchen and shatter every other day. I put it down to my tiredness, that was why everything kept slipping out of my grasp.

*

A woman went missing. Her name was Ashley, I thought about her all the time. I couldn't open any social media without seeing her face and the pleas for her safe return, the pleas for information, the pleas for security camera footage. My hair was the same colour, she was vaguely my height and build, this shouldn't have made it worse but it did. I became obsessive about what time the sun set so I could try to make it back indoors before it got dark. I googled the same question every day. *What time does the sun set today? What time does it get dark? What time does the sun—* Of course, on the days where I was working this was an impossible problem. My catering agency had a policy where, if we were there after midnight, a taxi had to be provided. A client dismissed a group of us, smiling, at 11.45. The waitresses tried to stick together, but I wasn't walking to the same station as the others, the waiters shrugged and walked off into the dark.

*

I went to the laundrette, there was only ever one woman working there at a time. I knocked on the door of the back office. She was always annoyed when I needed to swap my notes for coins and I needed to do this every single time I went.

'Is that okay?' she said as she handed me a handful of pound coins.

'Yeah, that's fine,' I said, I never bothered to count them. She had already gone back into the office and closed the door. The TV above the machine was blaring *Loose Women*, they were debating whether it was possible to forgive your man for cheating. I thought the conversation was both depressing and totally uninteresting at the same time. The problems began the second I opened a machine and began shoving my dirty laundry inside. I heard the voices of the women arguing on TV cut out somewhere above me, but I scarcely noticed, I was grateful for the quiet. I put my coins in but the last one got stuck somewhere in the mechanism, wouldn't fall backwards and start the wash. I slammed my hand against the top of the machine angrily a few times before I heard the clunk of it moving down. I sat down with relief and the machine started up. I closed my eyes briefly but when I opened them the laundrette was dark, the lights had gone off and the machines were making a clicking sound, every single one of them was running, every single one. Most of them were empty and making troubling broken-machine noises, even the dryers were

59

running and I panicked, wondering if this would somehow start a fire. The lights on the front of the machines were all illuminated but the overhead lights had gone out. The woman came bursting out of the office, she looked shocked and furious with me.

'What have you done?' she said, while I looked on, bewildered. 'What have you done?'

*

The Ashley case took over everything. I had been ignoring Helene, the immediate intimacy had scared me. I thought about her constantly but I had no idea what to say to her. My heart pounded whenever I pictured her but I was scared to go out after dark, all I did was go to work and then lock my door. I didn't want to tell her I had seen the man from the party, talking about it would make it real. I thought if I talked about it I would have to feel it, really feel it, and I couldn't do it.

*

My silence didn't deter her from trying to get in touch with me, she sent me strange messages, out-of-the-blue non-sequiturs about her day. **Portia being a total bitch at work, it's like, we get it, you're a ceramicist.** She sent one or two a day even though I kept ignoring them. Once she sent me a video. I was at home lying down and not falling asleep, spiralling while staring at my ugly ceiling. When I tapped the video I saw it was a short-haired black cat, it was winding itself around her legs affectionately. She was wearing a long floral skirt and the cat dipped in and out of it. Her hand

60

and wrist were in the shot, her fingers carefully kneading at the cat's little skull, fondling her ears. My blood rushed to my centre as I looked at it, the sight of her hand, her fingers, her wrist, was too much. I closed my eyes and kneaded my eyelids with my knuckles until I saw stars.

*

A couple of days later she sent me a video of a crow, its wings were all twisted around like a black peony. I couldn't see what the crow was doing until I played the video. The crow was holding a pigeon's legs in its claws. The pigeon was dead and the crow was eating its chest, pecking at it with its sharp beak. I couldn't turn away from it. She hadn't sent any message with it, I ran it through my mind, had she sent it to provoke me? Was she the crow? Was I the pigeon? Outside my door the footsteps ran up and down and up and down, when the scraping started I wrapped one of my pillows over my ears. The video ended but I watched it again, then again, and again.

*

They found Ashley's remains. A man was arrested. They identified her by her dental records. I no longer knew what it was that I was supposed to do. I felt manic, removed from my body, I stayed up all night making loaves of bread, watching YouTube videos about missing people who were found years later. The women who narrated these videos had calming voices, I was soothed by their descriptions of blood, mud, fingerprints. My hands and wrists ached, my head felt permanently dull and vibrating softly, like steel that had been struck. At work everyone had to yell their instructions twice before I heard them. There were vigils for Ashley. I was determined to attend. I called my friend Rosa but she was too afraid to come with me.

'Please,' I said, 'this is important to me.'

'It's too horrible,' she said, 'I can't think about it.' I sighed heavily on the phone, I felt like she didn't get it, what this woman meant to me.

'It's not as if you *knew* her,' she said. I didn't know who else I could call. I was desperate to go but I couldn't go alone, I thought about who I wanted with me. Finally I took a deep breath and called Helene.

'Of course,' she said on the phone, her voice was soft and sincere. 'Of course I'll come with you.' There were vigils across London but I needed to avoid crowds. I had to go to the one near my flat, within walking distance. She understood perfectly. She met me outside my local train station right as the sun was beginning to set. It was a stunningly beautiful evening, the sky was so blue, the light was so gold. I can hardly bear to think about how she looked in that light. Helene regarded me cautiously, a red cashmere scarf grazing her chin. I wondered how often she got her hair cut, I wondered if it was every month. I knew when we stood next to each other that I always looked worse in comparison.

'Where is it being held?' she asked. It was on the heath, outside a church. We had to walk up a steep hill to get there and I felt my thighs burn. There was a grassy patch of dirt outside the door of the church where a few people were standing around holding candles. The candles periodically blew out in the freezing wind and were attended to by a mousy girl in tweed. There were a few older women holding electric tea lights and a clutch of teenage girls all holding hands. I wished I'd brought something to hold, I had nothing to do with my hands. I looked around at the women there, there was one girl standing apart from the rest. She wasn't wearing a coat and her bare arms looked white in the blue light, her hair looked dirty and stuck down on her head and neck. Her face was turned away from us and I couldn't get a good look at her. I clenched my fists, my arms clamped to my sides. I felt my ears stinging in the icy wind. I thought I could feel Helene looking at me. I stood there for as long as I could stand to, the cold going straight through my polyester coat. It got darker and darker. My mind ran on and on, my anger was keeping me upright, I would have been too tired to stand without it, I could feel it running through my veins like petrol. It felt poisonous and chemical. I kept looking at the strange girl with no coat, slowly she turned her face to look at me. She was holding a candle and it cast strange shadows across her face, they looked like streaks of dirt. I smiled at her uneasily and her candle blew out, plunging her into darkness. I couldn't find her after that.

Helene snapped me out of my train of thought by prying my arm from my side and taking my hand. She nestled her head on my shoulder. She always smelled like money, expensive perfume layered on expensive moisturiser, expensive soap, Jo Malone, Chanel. The scents were gorgeous, I wanted it and hated it at the same time. I felt grimy next to her. She looked up at me and I realised I had been clenching my teeth.

'Where do you live in relation to here? Let me take you home.' I wasn't planning on letting Helene come to my flat, knowing what I knew about hers. I was afraid for her to see the clothes on the floor, the crumpled sheets, the dishes in the sink, all within such close proximity to each other.

'I don't know. It's a mess,' I muttered helplessly, but Helene was already in assistance mode, pulling me away from the churchyard and the older women with their LED tea lights.

'Come on, show me the way.' Her hand was interlaced with mine but she was wearing leather driving gloves, it was a strange feeling, like holding hands with a mannequin. She walked ahead of me and had to keep stopping so I could show her which way to go. The sky grew darker and darker as we walked. By the time we were in my flat it was only lit by the streetlights outside, my lighting was a joke, the whole place looked sad. I apologised and apologised.

'Shhh, shh. It doesn't matter,' she said briskly, taking off my coat for me and hanging it up like it was her house and I was a small child.

'I'm going to the bathroom. It's down the hall,' I explained and ducked out, looking for a moment alone to assess the situation. *She's here now*, I figured, *she knows how I live*. When I came back she was washing the dishes, my bed was made, the blanket was folded at the bottom of the bed. For a moment I was hot with embarrassment then a wave of tiredness hit me. My body let its guard down around her, something in me physically responded when she was around. The lack of sleep raced up to me all at once and I started sobbing hard. I pulled one of my pillows down from the head of the bed so I could sob into it. I listened to Helene calmly finishing the washing-up behind me, she put my cutlery down on the draining board and pulled the plug out, I could hear the water draining slowly. She picked up my blanket and draped it over me, then climbed onto my bed and held me from behind, her skinny arm slipping around my waist, swaddling me.

'I'm here,' she said softly. 'Everything is going to be okay.'
I wondered if the recent news had been affecting Helene in
the same way it had been affecting me. I supposed she was
more practical than me, she reacted less emotionally to
everything. Before long we lay down together and I passed
into a deep sleep. My dreams seemed to be getting more
abstract and more lifelike at the same time. In that dream I
woke up in an exact replica of my room, but I was alone. I
was wearing some kind of white camisole, my hair was loose
on my shoulders. I ran to my kitchen sink, there was a knot
in my stomach. I felt those familiar wretches of nausea and
after four heaving attempts, I puked a perfect white snake
into my steel kitchen sink. When I was done spitting out the
tail, the snake made itself into a little coil and turned to look
at me with its beady red eyes. Helene woke me up by tapping
me on the shoulder and saying my name over and over again
quietly and insistently. I jumped when I realised it was her.

'Hey! It's okay,' she said, grabbing my arm, she looked
me in the eye then broke away. 'Oh my God, you twitch so
much in your sleep it's crazy. You're like when a dog falls
asleep and chases imaginary rabbits in its dreams.' She
slipped out of the bed and stretched her arms up.

'I don't know how to respond to that,' I said. I still felt
queasy from the dream.

'Ha! Stay there, I'm going to make coffee.' I looked up
and realised she was already involved in the process, she
had already found my coffee pot.

'What time is it?'

'Around eight.' She didn't look back at me, she was taking my mugs off the draining board and arranging them
near the coffee pot on the stove. I felt slightly hung over,
emotional and tired.

'I've got work later,' I said aloud to no one in particular. 'What time?'

'Like six I think? I'm doing the dinner rush.'

'Oh that's ages away. I'm supposed to be in at ten to receive some shipment of something big and shiny, I don't know.' She waved a hand in the air, when she spoke like this I suspected that her disinterest in her job was something of an act. As if she thought it was a little vulgar to try at something as meaningless as an assistant job. I was sure when she was there she was completely professional. She turned to face me, her back to the coffee.

'Sorry I just passed out, I haven't been sleeping.'

'I know, you kept posting pictures of your bread dough at two a.m.,' she said lightly, but I knew she was a little hurt. I sometimes forgot that Helene could see what I posted, and the Helene standing in front of me was the same person who saw what I was doing online.

'You don't need to apologise, if you can sleep in the afternoon before work it won't feel so bad.' She handed me a mug full of black coffee, I sat up and rested it on my chest of drawers.

'Thank you for looking after me,' I said. She shrugged.

'Don't mention it.'

*

Helene didn't use my shower, saving me the embarrassment of telling her I had only one towel. She had brought deodorant with her, she was wearing an unsupportive lace bralet, I held my breath and tried not to stare. She adjusted her makeup carefully in my mirror in the hour before she needed to leave for work. Her clothes were good enough that she could wear them to see me and then go straight to her job at the gallery. I also realised that she came and went as she pleased from her job, the gallery seemed not to mind what hours she did as long as her basic duties were completed, the shipments received etc. Her unstructured time made me nervous. I wondered what she did with the rest of her day. While she got ready she regaled me with stories of the gallery, she was happy to monologue while I smiled and nodded.

'I had to ring up and order more champagne from the supplier, it's this wine shop that's only a few streets away, right? I ring them up and start telling them what crates we need. I'm decoding Octavia's handwriting which is awful and the guy is like, wow I really like the sound of your voice. Can you believe that?' I nodded, I couldn't believe it.

'Anyway he starts trying to ask me out. I tell him you don't know what I look like, I could be totally hideous. He says maybe I'll bring the champagne over myself and we'll see.'

'Uh huh.' I was losing interest in the story because I couldn't relate to the situation at all, this happened to me from time to time when Helene talked.

'So now I have to hide every time a supplier comes, I buzz them in but I stay in the back office. Isn't that ridiculous?' I did, in fact, think this was a bit ridiculous.

'Maybe you don't need to hide, you can just put on a funny voice so he doesn't know it's you.'

'Thanks,' Helene said sarcastically. 'I'll bear that in mind.' A pause stretched out between us. I'd failed to react how she wanted me to but I couldn't understand what reaction she was hoping for.

'I'm sorry I haven't been texting you back,' I said. 'I've had a rough week.' I felt genuinely guilty, I hadn't processed that it wasn't just me thinking about her, she thought about me as well.

'It's okay,' she said without looking up. 'I mean, I was wondering if you were okay.' She put down her mascara and looked at me. I weighed up whether I wanted to tell her what had happened. Her eyes narrowed a little, for a crazy moment I wondered if she already knew what I wanted to tell her. I looked away and she carried on adjusting her makeup. I wanted to trust her, I thought about how she'd come over as soon as I asked, how she'd taken care of me.

'I saw him,' I blurted out, my voice tightening. 'He was a guest at this event I was working at.' She paused, then pressed her lips together.

'Oh my God. Did you talk to him?'

'Briefly, he said he wants to talk, wants to clear the air, can you believe that? Then I got overwhelmed and threw up again in the guest's kitchen. They had to deputise one of the guys to drive me back to the station. It was so embarrassing.' I wished I hadn't told her about the puking.

'Has he spoken to you since?'

'He sent me a message saying he wants to meet up and talk but I ignored it.' Helene picked up and put down her coffee cup.

'I think you should go,' she said lightly. I didn't say anything, I just looked at her. 'I want to know what he wants to say. Maybe he wants to apologise,' she said.

'Then maybe *you* should go.'

'I can't go, he asked you to go, not me.' She looked at me for a second, then folded her arms and looked down at her feet.

'I don't know if it's even going to help,' I said. 'What if it doesn't help, what if it just makes everything worse?' My voice sounded shrill, needling.

'All I'm saying is think about it.' She held up her hands. 'For me.' I just stared at her.

'I have to go to work,' she said, picking up her bag, pulling her jacket on. She reached out and touched my forearm briefly, I experienced a jolt. 'Text me later, so I know you're okay.' I nodded and said nothing, she walked out of the door.

*

For days on end, I didn't want to talk to anyone. I didn't want to get out of bed. I didn't want to change my clothes. I didn't want to shower. I didn't want to eat. The immoveable fact of my existence had become unacceptable to me. I felt like my body was a large piece of rusty machinery that I had to haul around and operate. Whole shifts passed by and I hardly noticed. At one point I touched the scalding-hot side of a steel pan with the side of my hand as I was reaching to take a full plate from the pass. When I drew my hand back sharply I dropped the plate and it shattered on the ground. The food was all mixed up with the shards on the floor. I stopped still and just stared at the mess. Dan yelled at me while I stood there saying nothing, he threw a ladle at the wall and I heard it vaguely clang. All this barely registered, the burn on my hand felt like a distant buzzing sound, it blistered and I felt nothing.

*

My whole body ached, there was something wrong with my muscles, I wondered if I was coming down with the flu. Helene left me voice notes, I watched them accumulate on my

69

screen. *Helene sent you a voice message. Helene sent you a voice message. Helene Helene Helene.* I was frightened to listen to them, I couldn't quite understand why. She felt too close and too far away at the same time, picturing her face made my blood churn, I couldn't handle it, I kept avoiding her.

Three days passed this way before I decided I should listen to them, after all, she had rescued me from attending the vigil alone. I was still frightened of her, how I felt. It seemed unbearable to want someone this much. I slunk away from the empty pre-dinner dining room where I had been folding napkins and searched for somewhere quiet. I turned the volume on my phone all the way up, it almost sounded like she was talking in my ear, I could hear her breathing heavily as she walked along, her heels marching in the background.

'I don't know why you aren't talking to me, I thought we had an okay time? Despite the circumstances. Well, I did anyway. I hope you're okay. Will you call me back sometime, please?'

My heart rate spiked when I heard her voice, her clipped accent. She'd had a nice time with me and then I'd run away, again. I thought for a second then decided I didn't need to listen to the rest of the messages. I tapped on the little phone icon next to Helene's name. She picked up on the second ring.

'Hello?'

'Hi, I'm sorry,' I said.

'It's nice to hear from you too.'

'I'm serious, I'm sorry for avoiding you, I do want to see you, it's just been a weird time.'

'Are you okay?' she asked, my voice sounded strained when I compared it to hers. I sighed deeply and closed my eyes. I didn't want to think about anything anymore.

'Where are you? It's quiet,' she asked.

'I'm talking to you from the dry goods cupboard.'

'Hmmm,' she said, 'what are you thinking about?'

'What's it like to eat a live oyster? I've never had one before. What's it like eating something that's alive?' I moved a hand over my thigh and to where the seam of my tights met my underwear, I ran my finger up and down it lightly at first, then harder.

'They taste like seaweed, sometimes copper.'

'Well, that sounds awful.' I could feel her measuring the effect of the physical descriptions on me.

'No it's not, it's amazing.' I thought about the taste of blood, I licked a small paper cut, on my other hand, I pressed the phone between my shoulder and my ear. I thought about Helene's fingers in my mouth.

'I should take you to New York,' she said, 'we can go to a restaurant full of mobsters wearing gold jewellery and I can feed you a steak. Would you like that?' I knew she was half laughing at me but I didn't care, I wanted it too badly.

'Yes,' I said. 'Yes, I would really like that.' My voice was breathy and two octaves higher than usual.

'Aren't you at work?'

'Yes.'

'So go back to work,' she said, and unceremoniously hung up on me. It was completely maddening but I loved her for it. I'd gotten scared and ignored her and she wanted me to remember that she was in charge.

*

I waited the whole shift for Helene to text me and tell me to come over but she didn't. I thought about her all the way home. When I unlocked my door I noticed the cold, it was icy, even compared to outside. I grasped for the light switch, when the dim bulb illuminated I thought the flat was full of smoke. I stepped back in shock, then wafted my hand through it. It felt cold and wet. It was slightly dirty looking, the colour of a bedsheet that's been washed too many times. The smoke felt like fog, it settled damply on my skin and condensation ran down the windows. I unlocked them and opened my windows as far as they would go, I watched as the fog drifted slowly out into the evening. *What the hell?* I thought. *What the hell* was *that?* I sat down on my bed, still wearing my coat, and took out my phone, calling the only person I wanted to speak to. Helene picked up on the third ring, she was calm, she thought I needed a dehumidifier.

'My friend lived in a flat that was damp all the time like that. She had to turn on the dehumidifier every time she wanted to dry her clothes.' I dried all my clothes in the tumble dryer at the laundrette, it would have been useless to try and dry anything in the flat, it was too small and too cold. In the winter not even my hair dried on its own, it sat damply on my neck for days.

'You don't understand, it's like there was a big *wall* of fog in the centre of the room. I thought the place had caught fire while I was out but it's all cold and wet.' The fog had mostly drifted out by this point. My windows had cold evening air rushing through them and the traffic on the road outside was deafeningly loud, police cars, endless ambulances.

'What's that noise?' Helene said.

'It's the road outside,' I explained, a little embarrassed. 'I opened the windows to get the fog out.'

'But it's just so *loud*.'

'I'll close the windows, hang on a second.' I got up and shut them and made certain they were locked by jiggling the handles. I didn't tell her about how when the lorries drove by the whole building shook and my windows rattled. In the summer when it was hot and I had to have the windows open at night it regularly jolted me awake, it made me feel like the building was made of cardboard and a strong gust of wind could knock the whole thing down. Helene listened to me locking the windows and waited patiently for me to finish.

'Why don't you come over here tonight?' I considered this for a moment. It was cold in my flat and dimly lit.

'Okay. I'll be there soon.' She hung up without another word, my phone made a little purring sound in my ear. I looked at it and I had a little notification from the online payment service I used sometimes. She'd sent me £50, more than what a car ride to her flat would have cost. I made a mental note to file some of it away for later, in case I needed something urgently. I was agitated during the whole journey over there, I felt too hot and too cold at the same time. I took my jacket off then put it on again.

*

Helene buzzed me in, she didn't open the door herself, she left the door to her flat ajar for me. She was curled up on her couch flipping through a heavy, glossy magazine.

'I think we should order pizza,' she said. She didn't look up as I entered.

'Yeah, that sounds great,' I said, flopping down on the sofa, next to her. I let her choose the place she wanted to order from, let her pay for a large pizza and a bottle of wine.

'I'll have whatever you want to have,' I said. I felt confused and frightened when I was away from her but when I was with her it was different. When I heard the sound of her voice, a sort of calm sat heavily on me like a wool blanket. It was not the calm of contentment or even of happiness; it was the calm of someone awaiting an instruction with total confidence that the instruction would come. She was mysterious, unpredictable, and intense. She seemed to want me near her, but she didn't seem to mind when I didn't respond to her messages. She seemed content to wait for me to need her, she knew I would need her eventually. I couldn't stop looking at her, but when she looked back at me I became shy and looked away. I drank two glasses of wine and ate slightly less than half the pizza, not even food troubled me when I was with her. We talked about the weather, her job, and a coat she wanted to buy. She showed me a picture of it on her phone then quickly took it away again and locked it. I had a third glass of wine. I got up to go to the bathroom, I sat down on the closed toilet feeling slightly dizzy. I rested my head on my arms, my face was hot and I felt a little damp like steam bloom on my cheeks and forehead. When I looked up again to take a deep breath I almost cried out. Helene had a white fluffy bathmat, it was dense and white. There was a thick bloodstain in it, the blood was rich and viscous, it was a big smear like something bleeding had been dragged across it. The bathmat had been folded over on itself, in a haphazard attempt to cover the stain. I sat up straight, my heart thudding in my chest. My impulse was to unfold it with my foot so I could get a better look but I couldn't bear to touch it. I recoiled and drew my legs up to my chest. Suddenly I had to get out, I left the bathroom and ran into Helene in her hallway.

'Why is your bathmat all bloody?' I said it too loudly, she looked totally implacable, her emotions rarely registered on her face, the most upset I'd ever seen her was when she looked pained, irritable.

'Because I've been cooking.'

'You what?'

'I've been practising.' She ripped open the heavy door of her fridge and pointed inside. It was full of packages, things wrapped in greaseproof paper and twine. I was horrified, for a second I raised my hand, as if I was going to reach inside of the fridge and pick up one of the parcels. I put my hand down again and tried to think.

'I've been taking a class. I'm learning how to cook, so far they're only really letting us spatchcock chickens, and I already know how to do that, you have to cut along the backbone and remove it, then you flatten the breastbone with your hand.' She shoved the heel of her hand forward to show what she meant. There was an itch in the corner of my brain, a feeling of doubt, something about it didn't seem right, I knew that.

'So I've been doing my own research.' She smiled at me. 'I won't show you what I've done,' she said, she laughed a brief cruel little laugh. 'I know you don't eat meat.' I could feel her watching me. 'You're too good.' She closed the fridge in front of me, I felt her hand on the back of my arm, her fingers were cold, icy even. I turned to look at her and her face was flushed too, her eyes glittered. Her hand slipped into mine, her fingers meshed with mine and I felt the suggestion, the feeling of her pulling me towards her. My panic didn't recede, but a thought bloomed in my mind, *I don't want to know. Whatever she's doing, I don't want to know about it.* She watched me think. Not for the first time, I wondered if she could hear my thoughts.

'Stay here tonight.'

'I've got work in the morning,' I managed to say.

'So do I, and we're much closer to your work here than you would be at yours, right?' Her hands were on my hips, they moved towards my waist. *That's right*, I thought, *she knows where I work, where I live, she knows everything.*

'Yeah, you're right,' I swallowed. 'You're right.'

'Oh,' she said, she moved her hand up and brushed my hair out of my face, 'bunny, did I scare you?' Her hand slipped down a little to my jaw. 'You don't ever have to be scared around me.' She pulled me out of the kitchen and back to her room, I followed her without another word, utterly confused, completely willing. I hadn't felt so completely inside my own body in such a long time. I was so completely aware of what was being asked of me, what I needed to do and how to do it. I could hardly bear the reality of it, of her kissing me, of me kissing her. I had to imagine her out of this context. As I kissed her neck, I imagined her as she was when I first saw her, looking down at me in the bathroom with a nosebleed. As I felt her tighten and throb around my fingers I imagined her breaking down an animal carcass, raising her skinny arms to swing down a cleaver.

*

I fell asleep on one side of her enormous bed. I dreamt that I was locked in a room with the man from the party. Everything in the room was lush and white like it was an expensive hotel room. The door was locked, I couldn't get out. I got the sense that I had been locked in the room for some time, I knew this in the way that in dreams you know everything. I knew the nightdress I was wearing wasn't mine. I didn't know where the clothes were that I had been wearing when I entered the room. In the dream a great deal of time had passed. Every night in the dream he hurt me, there was a metal key that he used to lock the door and every night he slept with this metal key under his tongue. The idea was, I had to fetch the key from his mouth without startling him into swallowing it. I watched my pale hand in the dark, moving towards his mouth which was slung open in sleep. I woke up with my fists drawn up to my chest, afraid of his teeth closing over my fingers. I was scalding hot all over and slick with sweat. I slipped out of bed and went into Helene's bathroom. I took an icy shower, the shock of the cold water felt good, like it could make the dream disappear. I dressed hurriedly and went to work before Helene could wake up, it was still dark outside, the light was bleeding back into the world only imperceptibly. I thought it would probably be dark all over again by the time my shift was over.

*

When I got to Veau the kitchen was empty. The lights were all on and there was steam gushing out of a few pots on the stove.

'Hello?' I shouted into the empty kitchen, the door swung open behind me and I jumped, it was Eva, looking irritable.

'We're in the dining room.' She left again without bothering to explain. The whole team was standing around in a clump, I couldn't see over Noah's shoulder to see what the fuss was all about. He had the sleeves of his chef whites rolled up almost as far as they'd go and his arms were crossed. There was a man in a suit addressing the whole group. I assumed he was someone important because even the chefs were letting him talk without interrupting him.

'You seen this, Princess?' Noah muttered out of the corner of his mouth. The man in the suit was standing in front of a circle of chairs, the chairs were all stacked at improbable circus angles, piled high, it looked fragile. I stepped back slightly, afraid the whole thing could topple over at any moment.

'I don't know if there are people here who think this sort of thing is funny. But we will not tolerate practical jokes of any kind. You are now dismissed. Eva, stay here and help me set up for breakfast.' The clump started to disperse.

'What happened? I missed the start of the meeting,' I asked Noah furtively.

'Nothing, nothing. Someone decided to fuck with the furniture that's all, they think one of you lot did it as a joke. You know, make it look like the chairs in *Poltergeist*.'

'You shouldn't joke about that,' Eva said as she pulled down a chair. 'Taps were on all the way in the ladies as well, it flooded and the lino's gone mouldy.' *In one night?* I thought. I felt anxious. 'It's some kind of presence, someone's brought something in with them, there's something here, following them around.' Noah clapped his hand down on my shoulder and I let out a shriek.

'Woah! Princess, hey it's just me, it's just me.'

'That's not funny.'

'It's just me!'

'I know, just, it's not funny, stop it.' I wriggled from under his grasp and walked out.

'So touchy!' he shouted after me. I walked out of the room and locked myself in a cubicle in the flooded ladies' toilets, there were still puddles of water that hadn't dried on the floor. I could see the edge of the lino peeling away slightly from the skirting board and I kicked at it with my foot, there was black mould underneath it. *There's mould everywhere in London*, I thought, *that's all it is, and the chairs are a joke, someone's messing with Eva, because they know she believes in this sort of thing.* I sat there for a few moments until I felt the tension lessen in my shoulders, then I got up and went back into the kitchen.

'Princess, I've got something for you.'

'Oh yeah, what is it?' I said without turning around to look. I could hear the smirk in his voice already.

'Always so suspicious, come and look.' Noah and Dan, one of the other chefs, were standing around a hunk of meat and a huge knife. 'Beef carpaccio,' he announced.

'Gross,' I said appreciatively. Dan rolled his eyes and tutted.

'I'll give you ten quid if I slice you off a piece and you eat it.' Dan looked horrified.

'This is expensive shit,' he said darkly. 'People pay *us* for it.'

'Twenty,' I said.

'Done.' I immediately realised I could've asked for more. He brandished the knife and shaved off a slice from the side of beef, arranging it on a side plate, I reached for it.

'Wait!' he said, drizzling it with oil and cracking pepper and sprinkling flaky salt over the top.

'Now you can have it.' He didn't give me any utensils, I thought it would be best to just get it over with, I pinched it like a piece of tissue, rubbed it around in the oil and shoved it in my mouth, chewing rapidly and swallowing. Dan made disgusted noises, the texture was gummy and strange, it stuck to my teeth, it tasted like iron. I swallowed and grimaced. I felt a trickle of olive oil slide out of the corner of my mouth, it felt warm on my face. Before I could react Noah reached over and brushed the trickle upwards with his thumb back into my mouth. I backed off in horror and swiped at his hand with my fists. One of my hands collided with his face, I thought I would stop but I didn't. I dug my nails into his cheek, the heel of my hands covered his mouth.

'Don't fucking touch me,' I said, I remember his face, close to mine. 'Don't ever fucking touch me.' My voice didn't sound like my own, it sounded like it was coming from across the room. I felt him struggle, his hands pushing against my shoulders. I shoved his head back against the pass, I heard it thud and walked out. In the bathroom I washed my mouth out with water from the tap until it didn't taste of beef or oil anymore. I looked at myself in the mirror, I pressed my forehead against the glass and breathed until it fogged up. When I looked up again the face in the foggy mirror wasn't mine at all, the eyes were milky and blank, the mouth yawned open to reveal a dark void. I rubbed at the mirror with my sleeve and my own face reappeared, I looked awful, my cheap mascara had pooled underneath my eyes. I took a breath and went back out of the bathroom.

No one in the kitchen spoke to me for the rest of the night, it suited me, I didn't feel like apologising. I didn't feel anything except disgust, the sound of his skull hitting against the metal grated on me like a fork on porcelain, I wished I could recreate it somehow, scratch the itch. When it was time to eat something Noah put some of the sides on a plate and left it on the pass for me. When I picked it up there was a £20 note folded underneath it and I pocketed it. None of us ever mentioned it again.

*

After what happened in the restaurant I started to think about the consistent factors, I made lists about the various incidents, the fog, the electricity in the laundrette. *I'm the problem*, I thought, *somehow all of this is me.* I considered tracking down a priest but I wondered if he'd make me explain my relationship with Helene. I did some maths and I had just enough money to pay a psychic for one hour. I found her by googling the words 'psychic near me'. The woman I chose was going by the name Psychic Lizzie, Medium and Visionary. She had eight five-star reviews:

> 'She greets you in her lovely, cosy home & makes you feel welcome immediately. Great experience! Thank you'

> 'In times of joy and sorrow, she has been there and helped me see things from different perspectives and has given me a better clarity on many people and situations'

> 'Brilliant and wonderful you have the gift!'

Lizzie didn't have a website, I had to call her on the phone. She picked up immediately and said 'Psychic Lizzie!' in a sing-song voice. I stammered:

'Hello? I need to schedule an appointment.' I sounded panicked and mousy.

'Where are you based, love?' It was often this way with older ladies, they were always trying to take care of me or tell me what to do, to guide me in the right direction.

'It's okay, it's better if I come to you anyway. I don't have any space.'

'Whatever you want, love. How about this afternoon, two o'clock? It's Flat 12 Lincoln Court, on the left of the park.'

'Sounds great,' I said. I had no plans, nothing to do for the rest of the day, I wondered how long it would take to figure out what was wrong with me.

'It's all booked now, make sure you bring cash, see you then, all right love?' I opened my mouth to respond but she had already hung up. I didn't tell Helene about the appointment, I thought she would think it was ridiculous. I took the money out of a cash point and shoved it in a flimsy paper envelope. I couldn't bring myself to write 'Psychic Lizzie' on the front so I just wrote 'Lizzie'. I followed the blue dot on the map until I reached her address. Her building was a lot more modern than I had expected, it was an expensive tower block, in a nice part of London. Lizzie's building even had a buzzer with video, I could see myself on the little screen. Psychic Lizzie was in Flat 12, I held down the button and it illuminated blue.

'Hello?' It was the same voice from the phone.

'I've got an appointment, two p.m.?' There was a pause. 'We spoke on the phone?'

'Is that you, love?'

'Yes, we spoke earlier?' I waited again.

'Who's that with you there?' I took my finger off the button and looked around, there wasn't anyone else on the street, much less standing next to me by the door.

'There's no one here, it's just me.' I pressed the button again and looked at myself on the tiny screen, it was just me, looking vaguely panicked and very, very tired. I was starting to get annoyed.

'I booked an appointment—' I said again into the buzzer.

'I can't let you in, love!' she said before I could get to the end of my sentence. 'I can't let you in like that!'

'What are you talking about?'

'There's something there with you and I don't know what it is but I don't want it in my house, I'm sorry.' She didn't sound sorry at all, *Crackpot*, I thought, *what a racket, she probably just forgot I was coming.*

'Can I at least reschedule?'

'Don't come back here! Don't contact me again,' she shouted into the intercom. I stepped back, and looked up at the tower block, *Waste of time*, I thought to myself. There was nothing nearby for me to do, nothing to make the trip worthwhile, so I took myself home. I lay down and watched sitcoms on dodgy illegal sites. I heated up a frozen pizza, I thought about taking a shower and washing my hair. Getting up felt painful and boring but I found the strength to do it. I came to and I was standing in the communal bathroom, the door was bolted behind me but I couldn't seem to remember why I'd walked in there. I hadn't bothered to pull the cord to turn on the light, it was dim, the only source of light was the streetlamp outside the window. It was unbelievably cold in the bathroom, I could almost see my breath in front of my face. I hadn't even bothered to put on my dressing gown like I usually did, I was wearing a cheap cotton dress I used to wear in the summer until the elastic started to sag around the neck and hem, I had been wearing it to bed. I walked over to the sink and looked into the mirror. There were two or three large smears across its surface, I guessed they were soap stains. Over my shoulder there was a shadow. As soon as I noticed it in the mirror I began to sweat. I tried to only look at it with one of my eyes, I felt acutely afraid of what I would find if I really looked. I couldn't quite perceive it, it was strangely liquid like electrical static. I looked a little more closely into the mirror and I still couldn't pin down what it was, and then it moved. For some reason, my hand flew to my mouth, clamping down hard on my mouth and nose. I could see it now, a head, bent low, a neck, the slope of shoulders, it was raising its head, trying to raise its eyes to look at me. In two steps I crossed the room and pulled the cord to turn on the light. I turned back to the corner where it was standing and there's a waste-paper bin, the toilet, nothing else was there.

*

The next day I woke up and began coughing. I was convinced there was something stuck in my throat. At first I thought it was dust because I never did any dusting, even the mirror I looked into every day was covered in its fine grey fur. Then as I kept coughing, I wondered if a spider had crawled into my open mouth as I slept. Nothing came out of my throat as I bent over in bed hacking and hacking until I couldn't cough anymore and I had to get up and start my day. Two days passed and the coughing wouldn't leave me, it only got worse. I spent several whole shifts trying to keep from coughing in front of customers. I coughed in the bathroom cubicle and emerged to find a customer looking back at me in the mirror, horrified. One of my supervisors found me in the walk-in freezer hacking into the crease of my elbow.

'You should get that looked at, it sounds awful,' he said disinterestedly. When I breathed in, my breath rose in my chest with a distinct rattle, like an old elevator moving on cables up through a building. I went to Helene's after work, it was late but she was still awake. When I told her about the coughing she rested her hands on my chest, feeling the way the air moved.

'You have to go to the doctor,' she said softly. 'You're going to get pneumonia otherwise.' She wrapped one of her scarves around my neck and secured it. It was navy wool, soft and warm, touching it felt like touching a live animal.

'Promise me you'll do this.' I promised her. Inside, I was too stressed to think about going to the doctor, getting time off work. I could feel the stress sitting in the front of my skull, I could almost feel it buzzing when I rested my palm on my head. I had to go back to my flat, change my clothes, decompress, she reluctantly let me go, I could feel her disapproval. The second I got through the door to my flat I removed a few items of clothing and crawled into bed. I fell asleep almost immediately and dreamt that I was throwing up clumps of black ink onto the cream carpet in the restaurant. *I'm so sorry!* I shouted in the dream. There was a crowd of customers looking on, they were smartly dressed, the men wore tuxedos, the women wore diamonds and had their hair piled high on top of their heads, no one stood up, no one tried to help. I stumbled and puked onto a white tablecloth, the black ink spread outwards, a beautiful woman exclaimed in disgust, her date looked on. I looked up, directly into his eyes, it was the man from the party, his hair had gel in it, he was holding a champagne flute, sneering down at me as I backed away in shock.

I woke up coughing again, I called the doctors as soon as they opened and they put me on hold immediately. I was still lying in bed listening to their tinny music when

I noticed a cluster of black specks over my white chest of drawers, like an accidental spray of paint. I got up to look at it more closely and I noticed a line of it trailed downwards behind the chest. I clutched the phone between my shoulder and my ear and wrenched the chest away from the wall. The mould was everywhere, a huge black mass on the white paint. I almost didn't hear the receptionist shouting:

'Hello? Hello?'

'Yes! Hello, I'm here. I need an appointment,' I said, shrinking back away from the wall, pulling the edge of my T-shirt over my mouth and nose.

'What's your name? Date of birth?' I recited them mechanically.

'I don't have anything for three weeks.'

'Three weeks? I don't know, I think I've got a chest infection, I can't stop coughing. I work in catering. I can't keep coughing at work.'

'If it's an emergency you'll have to go to A&E.' She sounded profoundly bored, extremely annoyed that I'd mentioned my health problems to her.

'Well I don't think it qualifies as an *emergency*. I'm not dying or anything.'

'Is the twenty-sixth all right?' I paused and realised she was talking about the date three weeks away.

'Sure. Why not?'

'It's all booked in for you now.'

'Okay, thanks,' I said bemusedly, she hung up the phone and I looked at it in my hand. I took some photos of the mould on the wall, close up and then further away. I sent a picture to Helene with the caption I think we've solved the mystery of where my cough is coming from!! I began drafting an email to my landlord, trying to come across as sufficiently polite and pathetic at the same time.

So sorry to bother you, I think there is a black mould problem in my flat and I thought I should notify you. Has this been happening in the other flats in the building? Helene responded while I was staring at the message. **Jesus Christ** she said, I watched the little dots moving as she typed. **Did you get an appointment?** I sighed deeply, tried to take deep breaths through my makeshift T-shirt mask. **Three weeks from now . . .** She started typing again. **That's fucking terrible!** I ignored it because my landlord had responded.

Nope. Just you. Have you tried bleach and water?

Well, I guess that's my plan for the day, I thought to myself. I felt suddenly stupid, of course I was going to have to deal with this myself. I pulled on some clothes I didn't care about and began to tidy my flat, moving the chest of drawers away from the wall in earnest so I could assess the damage. I moved everything I could into the centre of the room, away from the mouldy wall. I took another picture of it and sent it to Helene. **Look this is what it looks like with all the furniture moved.** I googled 'How to remove black mould yourself' and scrolled through some articles. I took myself to the big supermarket, the sky was grey and oppressive overhead, it was so dim it could have been any time of the day. I blew some money on bleach, gloves, N95 masks, and a dark and heavy glass bottle of cough syrup for myself. **There's no way you're getting rid of that yourself** Helene responded. **Also, it looks like a face?**

No way, Virgin Mary is it?

I'm serious, look! She had drawn over it in the messaging app with little red lines to indicate where the eyes and mouth were. I could see it now, it reminded me of a depiction of a saint, it looked devotional somehow, the eyes were rolled back, the face raised up, the mouth open but downturned. **Spooky!** Helene said. I tried to put it out of my mind, I put on some loud music, I opened all my windows, I took a swig of the cough syrup without bothering to measure it out. I put on a mask and some gloves, I filled a plastic washing-up bowl with water, I mixed bleach and water in a spray bottle and shook it up. I sprayed it over the edge of the mould patch and began scrubbing. By the time I stood back to look at my work the mould had been replaced by a huge wet patch. I took a picture and sent it to my landlord. *I've done my best to get rid of it! I'll have to let you know if gets worse. Thanks for the bleach tip!* I hated myself for being so nice to him but I wanted to show that I'd tried.

Fine. Let me know if it comes back he said, it was freezing cold in the flat with the windows all open. **Part 300 of the bleach saga** I texted to Helene, **I think I've got rid of it, but now all the windows are open so I'm cold.**

Fuck's sake, just come over! she replied.

No no it's fine, I've got work in a couple of hours. I wanted to see her, but the thought of travelling all the way across London was too much to handle. She started typing and then stopped again.

*

At the restaurant there was some kind of scandal taking place. Two of my supervisors were yelling at each other in the middle of the kitchen, the head chef was watching with his arms crossed, occasionally interjecting. Noah was pretending to fillet some kind of gigantic fish but was really watching the argument over the pass. When I pushed open the door to the kitchen no one turned to look at me except Noah, he had been having trouble making eye contact with me, and I hadn't been speaking to him.

'What's going on?' I asked as loudly as I dared, pretending to be re-tying my apron strings.

'Hatchet job,' he said, 'in the Sunday paper.' Cherie was holding scraps of the paper in her fist and gesturing with them, one of them broke free of her grip and fluttered to the floor. I could feel Noah smiling at me in my peripheral vision.

'Hey Princess, look' – Noah had his hand inside the fish's mouth, he was making its jaw move, he put on a high-pitched voice – 'fish are friends not food.' In spite of myself, I started laughing, but then I started coughing. I couldn't stop hacking, I put both of my arms in front of my mouth. Noah slapped my back between my shoulder blades a couple of times, hard, before he realised I wasn't choking. By the time I was finished my eyes were streaming. I raised my head to take a big rattling breath. Both of my supervisors and the head chef were looking at me.

'See, this is what I'm talking about!' Cherie yelled, I very much doubted that this was what she had been talking about. 'We can't have waitresses in here with the *plague*, can we? It's so fucking *embarrassing*.' I looked at her and she snarled. 'Go home for God's sake, come back when you're not going to spread germs to all the customers.'

'No no I'm fine! Really I'm fine.' My voice was strained, I needed the money, I really needed the money.

'I already spoke to her about this,' Harry said smugly. 'Go home and call us when you're better.' Suddenly I was tired, very very tired.

'Fine,' I said, 'fine.' I turned around and walked out without bothering to say anything else. I put on my coat, I was halfway down the road before I started to worry about what it all meant. I cried the whole way back to my flat, hot fat tears, I couldn't seem to stop. There was simply nothing else for me to do. My flat was still dim when I got back, but immediately I saw it. The mould had reappeared, the face was obvious to me then, its mouth yawned open in a huge scream.

'How?' I said aloud, my voice was hoarse, almost unrecognisable. I called Helene, there was simply no one else who I wanted to call. 'I sent you a picture, right?' I said, frantically, the second she picked up.

'A picture of what?'

'The wall, after I cleaned it I sent you a picture?' There was a beat while she remembered what I was talking about.

'No? You sent me a picture before?'

'Crap, I must have sent it to my landlord. Hang on.' I sent her the picture of the clean white wall from my camera roll. 'That was this afternoon, now this is it now.' I took a picture of the face, it looked even worse with the flash on, I sent it to Helene. 'That's not possible, right? There's no way that all happened this afternoon.'

'That is really weird,' she said thoughtfully, I could hear in her voice that she was looking at the pictures.

'What am I going to do?' I could hear the tears coming back into my voice again.

'Hey, don't panic, don't panic. You're going to come and stay here, and when you're here we'll send the picture to your landlord and he'll have to fix it. He needs an exterminator or something.'

'I'm ill,' I said miserably, 'they sent me home from work.'

'I know you are, just come here, don't be an idiot. I'll take care of you. I'll be waiting.' I didn't bother to get changed, I seized a few things and shoved them in a bag resentfully. My chest hurt. Crossing London again felt insurmountable but I didn't see what other choice I had. And I wanted to see her, I wanted to be in her comfortable flat, I wanted to wake up and see her. On the way over to Helene's I thought I could see the face from the mould everywhere. As if it was a bright light that was imprinted on my retina, I saw it in the reflection of the windows, in the faces of the other passengers. It was waiting everywhere in the edges of my vision. I was so exhausted, I repeatedly nodded off on the train, my head kept falling forward and hurting my neck. Every time I jolted awake the train had emptied out a little more, the screen over the doors had stopped show-ing the next station and was glitching unpleasantly. It was emitting a faint whine like a mosquito, it was bright white and blank one minute then blue, then various pixels went black until it died altogether. I didn't care, I could usually feel when the train was at Helene's station, like a pigeon, I always found my way. I dropped off and when I woke up again the fluorescent overhead lights seemed dimmer than before. I wondered why, until I slipped into sleep, when I woke up again it was very dark. I figured we were in a tun-nel. The interior of the train looked grey, only one or two of the overhead fluorescent panels were lit up. I stood up and peered over the back of my seat blearily. I looked down the length of the train, I couldn't see anyone else at first but then I noticed a figure getting up at the far end. I couldn't see them properly, their clothing was dark. They lurched to their feet as if drunk and started to stumble down the centre aisle of the train, grabbing the backs of the seats for support. They moved clumsily, they moved faster and faster down the aisle but I couldn't get a good look at their face. I started to sweat, *They're coming for me*, I thought, *they're coming towards me*. I stood up properly, looking the other way to see if there was anyone else on the train, anywhere else for me to go but the train lurched forward. I fell back hard into my seat and the lights flickered back on. Slowly I peered around through the gap between the seats but there was no one there.

*

When Helene opened the door and hugged me, she was so bony I thought I could feel our ribcages touching.

'You look so cute in your waitress outfit,' she said in my ear. *It's a uniform*, I thought to myself.

'Stop, I'm so ill. You're going to get my cough.'

'No I won't,' she said, 'I literally never get sick, not ever. Come in and lie down.' She stood aside to let me in and pulled the door shut behind me. I took off my shoes, my coat, my scarf, and piled these items on top of each other in her hallway. I headed towards her living room. I thought about how when I first arrived there with Helene it seemed like a huge space, far too big for one person, but now I realised that it wasn't so big, not really. My own flat had shrunk by comparison and felt like an impossibly small, unreasonable space for a person to exist in.

'Helene, I have to talk to you about something weird,' I said. I felt like a child, standing in front of her in my socks, pulling my sleeves down, I was still cold, I was always too cold or too hot, somehow I was always uncomfortable.

'Okay, you should sit down though.' I perched next to her. I breathed in and I felt the rattling movement in my chest.

'I feel like—' I faltered, I covered my eyes with my hands. 'I feel like I'm being haunted.' I felt so exhausted, I wished I could lie down. Helene put her hand on my shoulder.

'I know exactly what you mean,' Helene said. I looked up, she was a blurry figure, reaching out to put her hand on top of mine.

'You do?'

'Yes,' she said clearly, 'I think all of this can go away, it will go away.' I cried a little bit harder, she moved closer. Her voice sounded lower in my ear. 'It will go away if we get rid of him.' She pulled me towards her, my head rested on her collarbone, I could feel her heart beating steadily.

'One day you won't think about him at all anymore. You'll feel completely different. One day your sadness will end.' I continued to cry. 'I can make this all go away, I'm going to take care of it. Do you understand?' She tipped my face up, I was looking into her eyes, they were so dark, I was falling down and down. I nodded.

*

I had no money coming in but it hardly mattered because Helene took care of everything. The first day after I was sent home I woke up in my usual cold sweat, convinced I was supposed to be there, but the panic soon passed and I fell back asleep. The next day I didn't wake up until late in the morning, and I didn't feel any panic at all. I sent a half-hearted email, asking Cherie when I could come back to work, she replied almost immediately.

Do not come into the restaurant if you are still coughing. Call us in a week. I shrugged. The agency emailed over the catering shifts for the week and I didn't email them back to accept any of them. Most days, Helene went out to work before I got up. She always woke me up in the mornings getting ready for work, spraying her perfume, taking her clothes out of the drawers. I watched her moving around the room, getting ready for the day. We didn't speak, she didn't like to talk in the mornings. Once she was done with her makeup she sat in silence at her vanity table, scrolling and typing on her phone, then she would place it screen down on the table. She would put on her coat and look down at me in bed, then lean over and kiss me on the forehead. I would hear her footsteps going down the hall and the sound of the front door closing. I would open my eyes and stare at the ceiling, neither awake nor asleep.

When she was away at work I did almost nothing. I was afraid to touch too many things in her flat, afraid of contaminating them somehow, moving them out of place. She bought me a nightdress, when she left me alone with it I checked the label and found out it was real silk. She'd tried to guess my size, it stretched tight over my hips and stomach but the straps slipped off my shoulders and the material slid around on my chest. When I put it on she looked me up and down and said:

'Perfect.' It was a pale shade of cream, I thought it made me look even paler.

'It's so nice,' I said, smoothing the wrinkles down over my hips. She was lying in bed, holding a book open on her lap, regarding me appraisingly. I picked up her phone to check the time and she leapt up.

'What are you doing?' she said, ripping the phone out of my hand.

'Nothing!' I said. 'I just wanted to check the time.'

'It's ten thirty,' she said. She got back into bed, put the phone back where it had been on her bedside table and started reading again.

'You didn't have to get this for me,' I said, trying to draw her attention back to the nightie. She closed the book and put it on the bedside table.

'All your clothes smell of damp or fryer oil.' She smiled at me then turned the lamp off, plunging me into darkness.

I started to do small things around the flat to amuse myself. I kept her kitchen spotlessly clean, I took baths with her expensive salts, and watched old films on her enormous TV. The sound of the actors moving across the screen distracted me, they were almost life-size. I made her dinner using her beautiful pans, I lit her dinner candles with an old lighter I found in the bottom of my bag. I made a thick sauce, cooking down tomatoes with onions and garlic. I chopped black olives and capers on a wooden board. I rolled up basil leaves and cut them into ribbons. I stirred yoghurt with salt and crushed raw garlic in a small pottery dish, arranged it with a teaspoon so it could be drizzled artistically through the pasta and sauce.

'What did you do?' she asked when she got in from work, pushing the strap of her tote bag off her shoulder.

'I made dinner, I wanted to do, y'know, something.'

'You're supposed to be resting,' she said, reproachfully. I took her coat from her shoulders and hung it up in the hall. I loved touching her clothes, they had weight to them, heft. When I walked back into the kitchen she was sitting down, sipping her wine and moving her pasta around the plate.

95

'So,' she said, expertly turning the tagliatelle around her fork, 'do you like being my wife?' I knew she was mocking me but I didn't flinch and she didn't smile. A blush spread over my face. Her cutlery was heavy, I dropped my knife on the floor and the clang was deafening. I bent down to pick it up, when I raised my head from under the table my face felt hot.

'Clumsy,' Helene said softly. She reached over and smoothed my hair, it was sticking up. The static shocked her and she drew her hand back. As soon as she withdrew her hand I heard a crash behind her. One of Helene's ceramic bowls was smashed into pieces on the kitchen floor.

'Where did you put it?' she said, getting up to survey the damage, turning on the light. I moved to help. 'Stay there,' she said, putting her hand out. 'You're not wearing shoes.' I got afraid for my bare feet, thinking about the tiny shards of the bowl, unsure of what to do, I sat down again.

'Just on the draining board. It wasn't precarious or anything, that's so weird.' Helene picked up shards of the bowl and wrapped them in a newspaper she'd discarded on the counter. She carefully pushed the package down in the bin and then swept up the smaller pieces with a dustpan and brush.

'I'm sorry,' I called out to her in the kitchen, unsure of what else to say. 'I didn't know it was unsteady. Oh no.' I looked down and Helene's glass had toppled over. A dark pool of red wine spread over the table. She walked over to me and looked down at the spillage.

'Why don't you just go and sit down?' I decided to do as she said, I blew out the candles and curled up on her deep sofa, drawing my knees up to my chest, making myself as small as I possibly could. I could feel her annoyance, I felt hypersensitive to her moods. Her moods were starting to feel like my moods, I was starting to look to her for cues about how I should behave. I felt a headache coming on, I closed my eyes for a moment and when I opened them the flat was completely dark. I heard Helene say my name into the soft darkness. It was much quieter at her flat than it was at mine, when cars turned down past her windows they quickly went silent and dark, her neighbours were respectful.

'Hello?' I said into the nothingness, I heard her moving across the room. Something cold touched my thigh and I flinched and cried out.

'It's okay! It's okay, it's just me,' Helene said, taking my hand. Her hands were so cold. 'Thank God I got all the shards swept up before the lights went out.' My eyes adjusted to the dark, I could see her eyes glinting back at me, she interlaced her bony fingers with mine.

'Let's go outside, I need to see whether it's the whole street.' She got up but didn't let go of my hand, she pulled me along and opened the front door. She was right, the power had gone out all down the street, one by one, the windows were all dark. Her hand tightened around mine.

*

The next morning, the lights came back on as mysteriously as they had gone out. I could hear Helene going around switching them back off. The bedroom door swung open and she looked down at me.

'Oh! You're awake. Good. What are you going to do today?' There was another psychic I wanted to visit, I had seen one with a shabby sign a few streets away, but I didn't want to tell Helene about it.

'I thought I might run some errands, take my laptop to a cafe, apply for some jobs.' She waved a hand dismissively.

'Don't worry about that too much. Something will turn up.' She stepped over to me and touched my face with the back of her hand.

'I might have to take a meeting here later. Around three?'

'Okay, I'll make myself scarce.'

'No no, I just don't want you to feel awkward.'

'That's okay, I'll be out.'

'Thank you.' She leaned forward and kissed my cheek, then my jaw, then she opened her mouth and briefly held my jawbone in her teeth, biting it gently as if testing if it would crack. I exhaled hard, this need for her always moved inside me, barely below the surface. I moved my hand to the back of her neck, running my thumb down the tensed muscle, then buried my fingertips in her hair, pulling her closer. It was no longer enough to move my fingers or my tongue inside her, I wanted all of her to swallow all of me. I had visions of her sinking her teeth into the soft part between my neck and shoulder, drinking my dark blood in great gulps, I closed my eyes. She released my jaw from her teeth.

'I'll see you later,' she said. She pressed her thumb to my lips and then she was gone.

*

Just as I'd promised, I was out of the flat before Helene's meeting. I walked past a little boutique with flowers outside. I bought a small and expensive bunch of blue flowers wrapped in brown paper, and I walked through a cold and silent park. The ground was stiff with ice, even the grass didn't relent under my feet. The nerves were back, acid rose in my throat, I felt overwhelmed by a strange fear. I tried to trace its source. I sat on a cold bench where the glossy paint was flaking off in thin strands. I watched my breath steam in front of my face for a second. I turned my face up to the sky, it was incredibly white as if starched. I shut my eyes tight, my chest tight with anxiety over the words passing between Helene and the other person, whoever they were. When I tried to picture her face I felt cold. I tried to list internally all the things that scared me more than Helene. I thought about deep sea animals the most, giant squid, things with tentacles and enormous eyes, the beach-ball-sized jellyfish I'd found dead on the sand as a child. They gave me the most visceral reaction, the weird throwing sensation in my heart when I thought about them moving through the ocean.

I couldn't think about men who were violent to women, it was too general, I had to get into specifics. I thought about a news story I'd read about a man who had kidnapped girls and kept them locked in his home. *That won't happen to me because I would never go into a basement with a strange man ever*, I thought. It was strangely relaxing, the horror followed by the relief, I knew that Helene would never do anything like that to me, as far as I could tell, it wasn't something women tended to do to each other. At least, I'd never read about anything like that happening before. I wondered how to spend the rest of my day, I scrolled through my phone, read an article or two about how quickly the world was ending. I wasn't really paying attention, I was mainly thinking about Helene. The more I thought about her the more I wanted the man from the party to die. The two desires had become tangled up in each other like two unravelled bundles of wool. It was partly my need to prove how I felt about her. I sensed her doubting me sometimes, her eyes watching me when she thought I wasn't paying attention. I wanted to tell her *yes I can do it yes I will do this for you*. My rage, my passion ran parallel to each other, they were the same hot geological spring. All I wanted was to be wanted by her, all I wanted was for him to die, to be obliterated, for him to never to be seen or heard from ever again. I knew Helene felt the same, I could feel the hot anger inside her, I could feel how good I made her feel, her thoughts were my thoughts and mine were hers. When we finally had to go to sleep I always told her to meet me in my dreams but when I fell asleep my dreams were as disturbing as they always were, and Helene refused to appear.

*

I walked further away from the flat, looking for anything else I could bring home to her. The shops sold gifts that were prohibitively expensive but I still went in and touched some of them. I picked up and put down heavy glass candle holders, ceramic plant pots. Once I realised there wasn't even anything small that I could afford to buy I turned around and walked out. I felt my phone buzzing in my pocket, it was Helene.

'All done, you can come back now,' she said. I shifted the bouquet in my arms until I was cradling it, and headed back towards her.

*

When I walked in the door the flat smelled different. It didn't smell of cooking or Helene's perfume or her detergent but there was another smell, some kind of soap, it was both strange and familiar like the smell of a clothes shop I used to go to as a child. The air felt thick, like there was someone standing just out of sight, waiting for me.

'There you are.' Helene came out of the kitchen and strode towards me. 'Are those for me?' I was still holding the bouquet, by its stems, I'd frozen in the act of holding them out to her.

'Er, yes of course.' Something was wrong, Helene's face was flushed, she ran a hand through her hair distractedly.

'Is there someone still here?' I asked.

'No,' she said immediately. I was still holding the bouquet, I moved it slightly back towards myself.

'I'm going to put these in water,' I said. Helene stepped in front of me.

'Why don't I do that?' She reached out to take the flowers from me.

'No, it's fine I'll do it.' When I stepped into the kitchen I felt the wrongness, it was in the atmosphere, I felt my heart pounding and I didn't know why. There were two mugs on the table, the handles at slight angles like the hands of a clock.

'He was here, wasn't he?' I said, as I said it, I knew it was true.

'No. Who are you talking about?' she snorted.

'You know who I'm talking about,' I said, I realised I was blindingly angry, it was as if I'd been suddenly and wilfully struck in the face.

'You brought him over here, didn't you?' I said. Helene said my name and sighed deeply. I dropped the flowers on the table and walked out of the kitchen and into the bedroom. I gathered as many of my things as I could and shoved them deep in my rucksack. Helene called out to me again, she stood in the doorway watching me pack, she bit her bottom lip primly.

'There's really no need for you to go.'

'Yes there is. I can't be here. You shouldn't have asked him over here, what was the point of it? You knew it would hurt me.' I could hear the tears thickening my voice, a heavy hardback book slid off Helene's shelves and fell to the floor with a thud. We both stopped to look at it.

'You're doing it again,' she said.

'Doing what? That has nothing to do with me.' Two more books fell, the lights flickered and made a buzzing sound like a wasp struggling to escape.

'It's not me!' I shouted. The overhead light went out, a small lamp illuminated Helene across the room as she stared at me. She looked beautiful and strange, there were dark circles under her eyes, it drove me insane that I could never be certain what she was thinking.

'I'm helping you,' she said firmly, 'we have a plan in place. I'm gathering information, it really has nothing to do with you.'

'Me and you have a plan or you and him have a plan?' I said, she made a noise of disgust and walked out of the room. I heard her response echoing as she walked down the hall.

'There's no point in trying to talk to you when you're like this.' She said something else I couldn't decipher, I didn't feel like chasing after her to hear what she'd said. I swung my rucksack onto my back and buttoned my coat. When I came out of the bedroom she was standing in the doorway to the kitchen with a tumbler half full of red wine.

'Honestly, there's no need to get *hysterical*.' She looked up reproachfully. I was out of the front door before she could say anything else. I closed the door behind me and walked in the direction of the underground station. I was suddenly too angry to cry. Too filled with the sense that once again I was all on my own. I didn't really want to leave but I had to go. I couldn't be in the house with her, with the feeling that he had been there. When I arrived at the station, I decided to walk to the next one down the line. Once I got to the next one I suddenly became aware that I was starving and wandered into a greasy spoon. I was amazed that it had survived, surrounded by Starbucks and expensive brunch spots. It was late in the afternoon but I ordered a vegetarian fry-up. I threw my weight into a plastic chair. I drummed my fingers on the tacky surface of the Formica, I stared down at the flecks of grey and blue and white. I took out my phone but Helene hadn't messaged me, no one was trying to get in contact with me. The fry-up arrived on a huge wheel of white porcelain. I gutted the fried egg and ripped open the hash brown, sopping it in the yolk before plunging it into the ketchup. I stuffed bite after bite of the fry-up into my mouth. I imagined eating innards, eating guts, I was so hungry I couldn't eat fast enough. I felt sick and determined. *I hate him*, I thought as I scored a tomato in half, *I hate her*, I thought as I sank my teeth into the buttery surface of the toast. I ate and ate until there was nothing left to eat, just an orangey smear of ketchup and my cutlery placed neatly in the centre. I looked up at the clock on the wall and wondered what I should do. Where would I go, what would I do? I couldn't afford to move out of my mouldy flat, I didn't want to go back to Helene's place. I tried to run through my options in my mind but my head began to spin. *Perhaps I will go to work*, I thought. I called Veau before I could change my mind. Cherie, my manager, answered. I could tell it was her immediately.

'I'm feeling much better,' I said, I usually sounded much more uncertain on the phone with her, much more apologetic. She let out a doubtful sigh.

'I've stopped coughing, listen, my throat's totally fine.'

'Well, we do need cover tonight. Can you be here at six?'

'Yes, of course.'

'It'll have to go on next month's payroll, it's too late for this month.' I did some mental maths and felt a brief jerk of panic in my chest.

'Yes, of course, that's fine.'

'See you later.' She hung up. The shift passed quickly because we were overwhelmed with customers, I simply did what I had always done. I focused on doing the job more than usual because I didn't want to think about the flat, about Helene in there with him. Why was he there? What was she doing there with him? What was she doing with me? I completed everything that was asked of me perfectly because I felt furious and I couldn't let anyone see the toxic feelings churning inside me. It seemed to work, after closing Cherie even looked up at me from her phone and said, 'Thank you for tonight.'

'No worries, I'm happy to be back,' I said, keeping my tone equally flat. I realised I wanted to scream.

'Hey Princess! Are you coming out with us?' Noah was putting on a jacket, there was already an unlit rollie clamped in his teeth. He asked me this every single time we got off work at the same time. I pictured Helene sitting alone on her blue velvet sofa, looking up at me as I walked in the door.

'Yeah. Go on then, yes.' I pulled my hair out of its strict bun, pushed it back from my face.

'Okay!' he said, he seemed surprised.

*

The pub the chefs had picked was loud and old-fashioned, the dark wood furniture was chipped, the slot machines glimmered in the background. I was nervous, I didn't know what to say to any of them. Eva was arguing with Dan about the relationship dynamics in a TV show I didn't watch. I couldn't hear the music clearly enough to comment on what was playing. I wanted to put my hands over my ears, to soften the noise. I tried to listen to them talk, I said nothing. Noah brought me a drink, I was horrified to notice I was the only person at the table he had bought a drink for. He wanted to talk to me but I couldn't separate the sound of his voice from the sounds of the music, from the sounds of every other person talking at the table. Finally one of his sentences broke through.

'Are you having boyfriend trouble?' he asked. He was trying to look sympathetic but had failed and was grinning at me.

'Something like that,' I said, and I felt acid rising in my throat. I took a big gulp of my drink, the ice hurt my teeth. I hadn't had a chance to eat anything since the fry-up, the alcohol was already affecting me.

'What do you mean?' he said, tilting his head to one side. I had strategically hidden this part of my life from the people at work before but something in me just said *fuck it, it doesn't matter now.*

'Girlfriend trouble,' I said in response, watching for his reaction.

'Oh!' he said. 'I didn't know. Are you a lesbian?' he asked, he looked visibly confused.

'No. Not exactly. I'm bisexual.'

'Oh!' he said again, his grin returned. 'Which do you like more?'

'What do you mean?'

'Like, if you had to choose, which one would you choose?'

'That's not – that's not how it works. I just like whoever I like, you know?' I considered trying to explain that not everyone I had been with would describe themselves as a part of either of those categories but the thought of talking about that to Noah gave me an immediate headache.

'But like if you had to pick.' Dan had been eavesdropping on the conversation and wanted to join in the questioning.

'Why do I have to pick, am I being held at gunpoint in this scenario?'

'Yes,' they said at the same time, I rolled my eyes.

'Fine, in that case I'd pick women.'

'I knew it,' Dan said smugly.

'Wouldn't you?' I asked Noah directly. He sputtered in response.

'Of course I would but I'm not, you know, I'm not interested in men.' I looked at him for a moment, certain suddenly that he actually was at least a little bit interested in men. He looked at me nervously and I smiled.

'Look, men are hot, women are hot, everyone sucks and that's the end of it.' I swallowed the rest of my drink.

'That's right!' Eva said from the other end of the table, pointing at me. I stood up and gathered my bag.

'Are you leaving?' Noah asked me, he suddenly looked puppyish, lost.

'Yes. Bye everyone.' The table made a mix of reproachful and jovial goodbye noises. On my way out I swiped a bottle of wine from a table where a couple were too busy staring into each other's eyes to notice, it was two-thirds full.

*

I kept walking around, taking secretive swigs from the wine, but there was nowhere for me to go. It was too late, there were no shops for me to stand in, nothing for me to do. The bars were too packed or had closed already, the streets were quiet except for a few drunk couples who stumbled past me, holding hands, eyeing me suspiciously. I walked and walked. I walked through a park, my heels scraping against the path, I saw something in the distance, lights and colourful bunting. I stumbled over the grass towards it, not even knowing what *this* was. It was a lido, there were white gates that were padlocked, I could see over the water, it shuddered and quivered in the wind. *Aren't they supposed to cover that?* I thought it was so strange, *They're supposed to cover it to stop leaves and animals from falling in, right?* Before I noticed what I was doing I had discarded the empty wine bottle and hopped the fence. I was standing at the side of the pool. The wind was freezing, it pulled at my hair and burned my ears. *I'm going to get in the water*, I thought. *I'm going to get in the water*. I felt completely calm, I did exactly as the voice in my head told me. I took off most of my clothes, I stood shivering in my vest and underwear until I couldn't bear it any longer, I half dived, half fell into the deep end. In the water I felt shocked, invigorated, horrible. *This was a mistake*, I kept thinking to myself, *this was a mistake*. I pushed myself down and opened my eyes into the blue. I could see something ahead of me in the pool, a white shape. At first I thought it was a seal, then a foam noodle, a buoy of some kind. I couldn't see it when I pushed myself up to look across the surface of the water. It was warmer under than out in the open air. I could see my own body under the water, it looked weak. I moved towards the object, keeping my eyes open. As I got closer I became convinced that it was a woman. She was face down, her hair fanned out around her head like a water plant, she didn't move as I thrashed closer to her, trying to reach out to her still body. I cried out unintelligibly as I tried to get close to her, pull on her. I couldn't touch her even as I moved closer. *I should get out of the water*, I thought to myself, *I should get out and then I can see where she is and pull her out*. I swam to the edge and hauled myself out, I stood up and the water fell off me, I wiped it from my eyes and tried to see. The lights around the pool were bright and stark, the pool was the same artificial aqua blue of every pool I'd ever been in. There was nothing there, it was all just blue, blue water, blue tiles. I looked and looked but there wasn't anything in the pool, I sat down on the edge of the pool, let my feet dangle in. I felt myself grow cold and I began to shiver violently. I pulled myself up. I put on my tights and jumper, pulling my coat around myself and buttoning it.

*

Once I was back on the path I began to run. I wasn't sure why, but I ran and ran until I was out of the park and back in a part of town with shops and lights and people. *I don't know where I am, I should get an Uber or something*, I thought, relieved to be having a mundane thought. When I took my phone off airplane mode a flood of messages stacked up on the screen, *Helene Helene Helene*. I swiped them away without stopping to read them, I typed the address of my flat into the app. I used the money Helene had given me to get back to my place. In the cab I felt exhilarated, it took about half an hour before I felt the cold. I realised I had run all that way and I hadn't coughed once. All the way back the driver was on the phone with someone he loved, he kept saying:

'Sweetheart, sweetheart it's okay, I know, I'll be home soon, it's okay.' When I got out in front of my building I was shivering. I unlocked my door, the flat stank of paint. My landlord had fixed the light, finally the flat was all lit up properly, the place looked so much larger than when I left. The rest of my belongings were all collected in the centre, even my bed had been moved away from the wall. The walls were so white they looked taller than before. I decided to go and have a shower, they had even fixed that too, they'd changed the showerhead. It felt hotter and the water pressure had improved. I stood in it until I felt warm again, I felt totally clean. I crawled into my awkwardly placed bed in the centre of the room, passing out until I was woken by Helene calling my phone. The first time I let it ring out and she immediately called me again: *Helene, Helene*. I shoved the phone under my pillow and waited for it to stop making noise. It petered out and I rolled over to face the wall, staring into the cold surface of the paint, trying to make out its texture. I took my phone out once it had stopped making its grinding noises under the pillow. I swiped away all the notifications from Helene before I could read them. My landlord had sent me an email, my rent was going up. He hoped I would be able to stay in spite of this *necessary increase*. I felt a wave of sickening anxiety and closed my eyes hard, it passed through me surprisingly quickly, it was out of my control. I didn't know how I could pay it, I could be forced to move on, they were trying to force me out. Something I had truly feared was happening and all I could do was shrug. I thought about Helene, her face, her shoulders, the back of her head. I thought about the sound of her voice and shut my eyes tightly, overwhelmed. Then I thought about the two mugs on the table, the thought of the man from the party and Helene meeting, talking together. My anger poured through me again, my face felt hot, my makeup had turned into grit around my eyes.

I swiped my thumb down over the screen and read her messages. At first she had been furious:

I can't believe you would just walk out like that.

Where are you?

This is so fucking childish, I can't believe you won't even talk to me.

After a while her tone changed:

Please just message me back so I know you're okay.

Where did you go?

Please just come back. She wrote it over and over like it was an incantation.

Come back.

Come back.
Come back.

*

I looked around my flat, I pulled the duvet tighter around myself. I typed out several sentences and deleted them. There was so much that I needed from her. I hated her, I wanted her so badly, I needed her to shelter me from the world. I opened the thread. **My rent is going up** I wrote, **I'm going to have to move.** I paused. **I don't know what I'm going to do.** My eyes filled with tears, I really didn't know. She started typing and then stopped again. I closed my eyes and balanced my phone on my sternum as I allowed myself to cry some panicked tears for a few minutes. My tears rolled out of my eyes sideways and I felt them dampen the pillow. When I picked up my phone again I saw that she'd responded. **Just come back here** she wrote, **please.** I held my breath for a second, I began to imagine all the different variables but I stopped myself, this was my only choice, really, I had no one else. **Are you sure?** I wrote. She responded immediately.

Of course I am. Bring everything, I want you to.

Okay I wrote. **Thank you so much.** She sent a heart, it glowed tiny and red on the screen.

It took a pitiful amount of time to collect my possessions, I didn't have much of anything. The things I didn't want went in a box that I put downstairs outside the front door, I wrote FREE on the front in felt tip, hoping someone would take it. I would deal with my landlord later, I couldn't stand to communicate with him any longer. The sum total of everything I needed fitted in an Uber that Helene had sent. When I arrived on her doorstep she said:

'Is this everything?' I nodded sheepishly. She adjusted her expression and stepped forward to kiss me hard, her fingers pulling at the hair on the back of my neck.

'Thank you for coming back,' she said as she pulled away. 'You don't have to worry about anything now.' We unloaded my things into a room I hadn't previously known existed, it was off the kitchen, a kind of dining room that Helene was using as an office-slash-storage-unit. The second we were done I wrapped my arms around her waist. All I wanted was to be close to her, I needed to make her feel good. My mind narrowed to a sharp point, I wanted my hands on every part of her, I wanted my hands to be in that place between her thighs that made her bite down hard on the soft part between my neck and shoulder. I looked deep into her eyes until her pupils almost eclipsed the irises.

Afterwards I was full of energy. I sat up in her enormous bed watching the parakeets dart back and forth in their hi-vis green feathers. Helene was awake too but she was keeping her eyes closed, her hair spread around her head on the pillow like a dark halo.

'Do you think they're an invasive species or do you think they get along with the other birds?' The parakeets screeched and screeched like they could hear us talking about them.

'I don't know,' Helene said, resting her hand delicately on her forehead. She hated to be disturbed when she was tired, she never complained but I could see it in her face, how she moved in the mornings. 'I read somewhere they've been here a lot longer than people think, since the nineteenth century. It was the Victorians who first introduced them.' She turned over so her back was to me. I made an inventory of the freckles on her back like I always did when she turned away from me like that.

'Hey,' I said to the blank space, the thick nest of hair covering the back of her skull. I reached out and touched her hair. I felt her stiffen. I pulled away and sank deeper into the bed until the duvet covered the lower half of my face. Sleepily, Helene rolled over again and pulled me closer until I was nestled against her chest, she stroked my tangled hair with her bony fingers.

'You just need to trust me, even when I don't tell you something, I have my reasons, and you can ask me what those reasons are, but only if you really need to.' I made noises of agreement even though I wasn't quite sure what she was asking me to do. She seemed a little hurt that I didn't understand her plan even though she'd never explained it to me.

'So, how do you see it?' I said haltingly.

'How do I see what?'

'All of it, what we're doing now, what happens next?' She paused.

'Don't worry about what's going to happen next, it's better if I tell you only when you need to know.' Something in the way she said it made me take her seriously, maybe I really didn't want to know.

'You don't know what it was like for me. When I was with him.' I moved so I could look up at her, into her eyes.

'So tell me,' I said. 'I want to know.'

*

His father was in business with her father, which made things complicated. Their parents didn't socialise, she and

he had become used to glimpsing each other only momen-
tarily from behind their parents. They didn't meet properly
until university and by that time an awkwardness had
grown between them, they didn't know how to talk to each
other. They were placed in tutorials together, which made it
all the more excruciating. He was insecure, underprepared,
having chosen the impractical, cerebral subject to spite his
own father. He would speak loudly and at length, making
grandiose arguments, seizing on the parts of the text that he
had read. When it was time for Helene to speak she would
turn her head to one side as if considering his arguments
then quietly, methodically, refute every single one of them.
Her hair had been longer then and she almost always wore
it drawn away from her face in a low ponytail. In one of
these tutorials their lecturer, Otto, had turned away to fetch
a book, when he reached over, grasped the middle section
of her ponytail and yanked on it sharply. He then calmly
removed his hand and placed it on the back of her chair.
She didn't make a sound but tears sprang to her eyes and
her face flushed from the humiliation of this invasive and
juvenile gesture. After their session he spoke to her for the
first time.

'No hard feelings,' he said, holding out his hand. 'Come
on, let's get a drink.' Helene raised her voice several deci-
bels above its average and shouted the word: 'Never.' She
allowed herself to angrily pace back and forth for exactly
ten minutes in her university room before completing an
essay, scrubbing her face with cold water and falling asleep.
It was around this time that he started to tell people that he
knew her, that they had grown up together. He told stories
about the Barbies she'd played with, about them sneaking
off together during family camping holidays. It was pretty

fanciful stuff, Helene had always preferred books to dolls and anyway her family would never have gone *camping*. It forced her to confront him. She had a few plastic cups of a mystery cocktail at one of their socials and shoved him in the chest.

'Hey!' she said, as he stumbled backwards, drunker than her. 'Stop telling people that you know me. You don't know me at all.'

'But I do,' he said boyishly. 'I've seen you all the time.'

'That's not the same thing, we've never spoken.'

'We're speaking right now!' he said. She threw her arms up in disgust and began to walk away. 'Why are you so mean to me with Otto?' Helene liked Otto, he was impassive, he was an older and calming presence, like a nice chair.

'What are you talking about?' she said.

'You never let me win. You win every time, just let me get something right.'

'It's not my fault you're always wrong, maybe you should try harder.'

'Pleeease, Helene,' he said, drawing out the e's like he was a child. 'Just, agree with me about one thing, once. I'll stop telling people that I know you.' She considered this.

'Fine. I'll agree with one thing you say.'

'OH, thank you so much,' he said drunkenly, before she knew it, he had swept her into a hug. His body was hard and hot against her cold softness. As soon as her heart started to beat faster she squirmed away from him and made for the other side of the party. A couple of days later she supported one of his grandiose arguments in a tutorial with textual evidence, and made it sound not so grandiose but actually rather radical and interesting. Otto nodded and made a note on his pad. At the end of the week they were seated together at a college dinner and Helene was uncomfortable. The man sitting across from her was a visiting professor, the man was pompous and cruel. Helene had tried to enter into the discussion that was taking place and this man had spoken to her in such a condescending and belittling way that she could not find a way to respond. She studied her napkin and clenched her hands at her sides. He had quickly and without looking at her slipped his hand into hers and held it firmly until the next course arrived. It was on this simple act of reassurance that Helene decided to pin all her hopes.

After that they were together all the time. He went from being excessively concerned with every girl he met everywhere to being excessively concerned with Helene and Helene only. Helene hadn't really had any close friends in school, at least, not those obsessive passionate close friendships women often have where they tell each other everything, their loves and hatreds, their jealousies and thrills. He became that for her, he was interested in her feelings, he wanted to know all her vulnerabilities, he loved all the ways she was different from that cold analytical person he sat next to in their tutorials. The tutorials became joyful, their debates tongue in cheek, as if they could never truly disagree. They laughed, they exchanged looks between the points they made. Afterwards the tension would break spectacularly and they would kiss passionately in the stairway that led down from Otto's office and they would walk away holding hands, debating whether Otto knew, whether he could tell what had come over them. It was lovely, it was like this for what felt like a long time.

*

It started slowly, as these things always do. She found it hard to get her essays done when he was around, he monopolised her attention. Her life had been highly scheduled before he was in it and now she was always playing catch-up, staying up late. He didn't like to watch her study, he would hover in her eye line, waiting for her to notice him. Once when she was in her room, determinedly ignoring him, trying to read to the end of a paragraph, he said:

'I don't like it when you disappear like that.'

'What do you mean?' she asked.

'It's like you just . . . go somewhere else altogether. In your mind.'

'I'm just concentrating, that's all.'

He paused. 'Sometimes I feel like you've got this house that you've built and it's full of these rooms that I'm not allowed into.' Helene pictured this house, she imagined it as a large pink dollhouse, when she looked inside she saw him in there, running up and down the cardboard corridors, trying all the doors but they were locked. From her vantage point she could see into all of them and he couldn't get through any of the doors. She smiled.

'What are you smiling at?' he said. She thought about telling him what she was imagining, then all of a sudden, she decided against it.

'Nothing,' she said. He stood up and picked up her stack of library books from next to her and threw them on the floor. They looked at each other. He wrenched the book she was reading out of her hands and threw it against the wall, then he walked out of her room. That night he appeared again as if nothing had happened, he had a bouquet of supermarket daffodils and a bottle of wine. He asked her about her day as if he hadn't yet seen her. He told her a funny anecdote about one of the men from his rowing team. His gestures and voices were expert and funny. Helene drank her wine, she laughed and nodded. When it got late he kissed her and said he was very serious about her.

'I only want to be with you,' he said, 'is that okay?' She said it was.

*

When they first got together she didn't notice the amount that he drank. He was too busy being with Helene, talking to her, making dinner with her. He slowly reverted to his old habits, if she came with him on a night out he was by turns excessively flirtatious and aggressive. She caught him, open mouthed, checking out other girls, or talking to them up close, touching their arms and their hair. She didn't like the role he'd cast her in, fun-vampire, spurned lover. If she didn't go he would come to her room when the night was over, no matter the time. The other students in her corridor complained about the noise and she found herself apologising for him, making excuses, as if it was her making the noise. He would bang on her door until she opened it, which she had to, if she wanted the banging to stop. Once inside he would try to undress her and if she resisted he would unleash a torrent of insults. He hated the way she dressed, the way she looked at him, she was withholding, boring, frigid, arrogant, she didn't emote like a normal person. Helene could not cry, she had very little to say in response because she didn't hate him like he hated her. She would try to reassure him, when he said she didn't love him she would say, *that's not true, that's not true* over and over.

She tried to get him to leave, pleaded with him to keep his voice down. This upset him the most, he grabbed her wrist, told her to stop speaking to him like a child. He hit her, slapped her in the face. Once or twice she hit him back, shoved him away from her. But he was physically stronger, she learned quickly it would be better not to react, to wait for it to be over, to let him tire himself out.

In the mornings he would try to make up for his actions. He would fetch her coffee, kneel next to her bed and tell her how sorry he was, how he was trying to quit drinking. How hard it was to be in that environment where everyone was drinking so much all the time. He would lay his head in her lap and cry until she had no choice but to say:

'It's okay, it's okay. I know you didn't mean it.'

*

They didn't just break up once, it ended repeatedly. He was always the one that ended it, he was emotional, he told her he hated her, he never wanted to see her again. Then a few weeks later they would run into each other somewhere in the small town and he would tell her how there was no one like her, how she was the only girl he had ever really loved. For a while they would be happy, happier than ever, then the cycle would begin all over again. Right before it ended for the final time he called on the phone and told her he was fantasising about her, his speech was slurred at the edges. At first she let it happen, she wanted to avoid an argument. But her thoughts stalled, she didn't want to do it. *I don't—* she said *I'm not sure—* her protestations didn't stop him, he kept going. Helene took the phone away from her ear and looked at it in her hand, she looked at his name and the numbers ticking up on the amount of time spent on the phone call. The side of her face was burning hot, the screen shining with sweat. She hung up on him and turned off her phone. Then she calmly, quickly, left for her year abroad in France. She was gone for the whole academic year and when the summer came around she stayed for that as well. By the time she returned he was in a different tutorial group and they lived on opposite sides of town. They treated each other as casual acquaintances, after all, they had mutual friends. Politeness was everything in their social set, no one ever did or said anything that might violate that unspoken contract. They both acted as if nothing had happened. But Helene's anger never subsided, it was with her forever, it pulsed through her, I could feel it, moving around. Her life was divided in half, there was the time before she had known him and the time after. She felt, on some level, that she had lost control of her life, that she had allowed him to happen to her. That whatever she did now, she would never be a person who had never been in this relationship. She would never again be a person that no one could hurt. She had been wounded by the experience, she was still wounded by it, and there was no recourse, nothing that could be done. This was a reality she could not, and would not accept. It was not a world she wanted to live in, and if she could not live in this world, she was going to make a new one.

Helene stopped speaking. I could sense her thoughts moving in her head, the different pieces shifting and connecting.

'How do you feel now?' I asked, she didn't respond immediately and I wondered if I'd said the wrong thing.

'I'm angry,' she said, 'I'm furious, every single day of my life.'

'Me too,' I said, 'I mean, sometimes I'm sad, sometimes I'm tired, but basically, yeah. Always.' She stared ahead.

'I never really wanted to hurt anyone before, not really. But ever since then I have had this feeling sometimes. It's like a form of blindness. I get so angry I feel like I could do anything. I get into this bright white rage where I don't care about anything, it doesn't even feel hot, it feels icy, like a freezing wind. I could do anything when I feel like that.' She paused again. 'I'm never tired. I'm either angry or there's just this quiet. There's just nothing.' She stared off into space, motionless. I wasn't really taking in what she was saying, I began slowly to fall asleep, even though I was resting uncomfortably against her bony chest.

'Don't accept any new shifts,' she said suddenly, I started awake. 'I'm going to need you here, just do the bare minimum to cover whatever you need to get out of your flat contract. I will take care of everything else.' I waited a second to see if there was anything else she needed to say.

'Okay. I mean, are you sure?'

'Of course.' She always said it like that, like she was offended that I thought she could be unsure about anything.

'I'll make sure to help around the house and stuff, and pay for any bills that you need help with.'

'I don't have any bills,' she said, 'everything's paid for.' I didn't ask by whom, I assumed her father, who she scarcely mentioned.

'Okay then, I'll cook.'

'Hmm,' she said. 'My wife.' She pulled a little at the short hairs at the base of my neck while I made appreciative noises. We shifted around until I was holding her against me, I fell asleep with my face in her hair. When I woke up in the night I sensed she was still awake in the dark. I woke up twice more and both times I was certain she wasn't asleep.

*

I only went to work at Veau after that, I ignored all the emails from the catering agency. As I was only there for a few days every week I had much more energy. After a few days of doing nothing but making dinner, I started to wake up early of my own accord. I could sense, however, that my presence was starting to grate on Helene. If I didn't make dinner for her she would ask what I had been doing all day, when I did make dinner there was always something wrong. My pasta dishes were oily, unhealthy. If I made a salad she would complain about how starving she was. When I made something she really liked, tahini, garlic and lemon noodles, miso salmon and charred broccoli, she would eat the whole thing then complain about the smell or the mess. I couldn't get the kitchen to look how she wanted it to look. Even when I had washed up and scrubbed the surfaces, as soon as I sat down she would go into the kitchen and move things around, I could never learn their configuration the way she wanted it, my brain wouldn't hold the information.

*

I felt dominated by her, I felt myself vanishing under her authority. I barely thought about anything but her, especially when she wasn't there. I walked around in a daze in her absence, wondering what I could do for her, when she would be home. I felt like I was always passing through someone else's cloud of cigarette smoke or perfume. Everything seemed powerful and unfamiliar. I buried my face in the hollow of her neck and counted the scents, Chanel, sweat, talcum powder, rusted metal, blood. I was lonely, but I'd forgotten how to reach out to my friends. Several times I typed out a message to Rosa and deleted it again, I didn't feel like explaining what had happened, where I was. I thought about food less now I wasn't at work all the time, my appetite almost disappeared, I only thought about Helene.

*

My panic attacks would not relent. Repeatedly I would get close to the point of coming, only to be seized by suffocating fear. I had to clamp my hands down on Helene's shoulders and push her away from me. My breath rose through my body in huge shuddering gasps. She kept trying to put her hand on my arm, my thigh, but the feeling of being touched made it worse. The only thing I could do was lock myself in her en-suite bathroom and sit on the floor until the horrible feeling had passed. I would wrap my arms around my knees and make myself as small and compact as possible. Often by the time I had emerged Helene had forgotten about me and fallen asleep and I would be left to lie awake next to her. One morning after I'd had one of my attacks she gently shook me awake.

'Did you knock something over?' she asked.

'No?' I said, too sleepy to be more polite and engaged.

'Come and look at this,' she said. I reluctantly followed her into the bathroom. I rubbed my eyes and I thought she had somehow disappeared but I looked down and she was crouched down on the floor touching the surface with her fingertips.

'Look,' she said. I focused and saw what she meant, the ceramic tiles were covered in little cracks, the cracks went from tile to tile, the problem had spread all over the floor like a spider web.

'How weird is that?' Helene said quietly.

'So weird,' I agreed. She went to work not long after and I was left alone again, I lay back down on the bed and stared into the ceiling, wondering what it all meant.

*

Helene's fancy neighbourhood was overwhelmed by urban foxes. As soon as it started to get dark they were all over the streets, roaming in packs of three. Most of them were healthy, they sprang from pavement to pavement, their tails bushy and strong, occasionally you'd see some poor sod with the mange or a limp, looking thin and grey in the shadows. Their eyes reflected light in that uncanny way where sometimes I would happen upon them tearing apart a pigeon or a takeaway box and they'd look up at me, a series of flat coins. They used to make an absolute mess of the bins, if the lid was left even slightly open they would practically upend them, tearing through in search of something to eat. When I walked around with Helene they'd scatter as soon as they saw her, fleeing into different hedges or slinking underneath cars. The strange thing was that they weren't the least bit bothered by me. Every time I walked back from the station after work they would turn their gaze on me and do nothing. I had to step around them on the pavement. *They know I'm one of them*, I thought, *they know I don't belong here either.*

*

I used to wander the neighbourhood, up and down the beautiful streets. One afternoon it was beginning to get dark when I noticed something blocking the pavement up ahead, I thought it was a jacket or some item of clothing that had been discarded. As I got closer I realised it was a fox. It was stone dead on the ground, its head had been bludgeoned, it was haloed by a pool of blood. I stepped back and around it hoping to get the image out of my mind, when I looked ahead and realised there were three or four more littering the pavement, all dead from a head wound, killed in the exact same way. Almost without thinking I took my phone out of my pocket and took a picture of them all covering the path ahead. When Helene got home I tried to show it to her, she was only half listening.

'Look at this,' I said, 'we should phone the RSPCA.' Her eyes flicked over my phone screen disinterestedly, then once she realised what she was looking at she grabbed my phone and stared into it.

'Ugh. Honestly that's disgusting,' she said, 'why would you take a photo of that, I thought you were a vegetarian.'

'I don't know,' I said, 'I suppose it just seemed too weird to be real.'

'Well,' she said, 'it certainly is weird. Maybe they all ate the same thing, you know, out of the rubbish.' I looked at her for a second, thought about pointing out their wounds then changed my mind.

'Yeah. That's probably what happened,' I said, locking my phone again.

*

She used to leave early in the mornings, it was usually still dark outside. I liked to hear her trying to keep quiet as she got dressed, put on her shoes. Before she left she would lean over and kiss me, sometimes she said *bye* in a whisper. Sometimes she wore lipstick to work and when I looked in the mirror the kiss mark would still be there in the centre of my forehead, a rosy cloud.

I would wait a few minutes after I heard the front door close, then I would put on my coat over my silly night-dress and open the heavy front door. I'd stand on the icy stone steps and look out in the cold morning for as long as I could stand it. I liked to look at my breath curling out in front of me and the frost on her tiny patch of grass. I was very interested in the neighbours, they usually didn't bother to close their curtains and I would sometimes watch them moving around inside while I waited for Helene to come home. There was an older man and a younger man, I could tell they were romantically involved. I hardly ever saw the older man because he left even earlier than Helene. I glimpsed a dark suit, a thin shock of greying hair. The younger man had the muscular grace of a dancer, he wandered around the house in his boxers usually, he didn't go out much. Sometimes he did yoga in the living room with the instructional video playing on full volume, sometimes he played pop music so loud I could hear it pulsing through the walls. On a couple of occasions he caught me looking at him when I came home, and sometimes I caught him looking at me. One morning when I stepped out on the cold doorstep he was on the adjoining doorstep.

'Hi!' he said brightly. I wrapped my coat around myself, embarrassed about standing outside in my nightie. He was wearing tartan pyjama bottoms and a cashmere jumper over his bare chest. 'Are you bored too?' he asked. I laughed uneasily.

'Yeah I guess,' I said. He looked at me quizzically but stepped closer, leaning over the railings.

'I'm Oliver.' We looked at each other. 'Do you want a coffee?' he asked, he looked a little shy. I thought for a second.

'You know, I really do. I'm just going to put some trousers on, then I'll come over.'

'Okay, great!' He beamed at me and I was surprised by how warm his smile was. I went back into the flat and pulled on some trousers I'd worn the day before. I put on a pair of Helene's slippers and one of her oversized luxury jumpers, which on me was about regular-sized. I went out of the door, pulling it closed behind me. Oliver's place had the same heavy door as Helene's, I knocked but I wasn't sure if he could hear. I waited a minute then pressed the doorbell's brass button. The noise was massive and grating. Oliver swept the door open looking surprised.

'Sorry!' I said. 'I didn't know it was going to be that loud!'

'No no it's not your fault. You didn't know.' He stepped aside to let me in and I paused in the dark hallway.

'The kitchen's straight ahead.' The kitchen seemed underused, the only sign that it was inhabited was the coffee pot and the open bag of grounds which was on the counter.

'Do you want milk?' I sensed a lilt of some kind underneath his neutral accent, a previous way of speaking that he was trying to conceal. I thought about the differences in the way I spoke depending on the situation I found myself in and I liked him.

'Oh no that's okay, I'm fine.' He handed me the mug and I took a sip.

127

'This place is beautiful.' I looked around appreciatively at the stylish kitchen.

'It's not mine,' he said with a shy grimace. I smiled at him.

'Next door isn't mine either.'

'I know,' he said, smiling back. 'Are we both kept women?' His eyes flashed, he really was beautiful. I wasn't attracted to him because I knew, somehow instinctively, that he wasn't interested in women but I admired him anyway, he looked strong and graceful, but not intimidatingly so.

'I do about three shifts a week at my old job, I'm still paying rent on my old flat.'

'I should have done that, kept my old place.' He sipped his coffee. I didn't know how to respond. 'What do you do?' he asked. I wondered whether to lie.

'I'm a waitress,' I said. He nodded, he wasn't surprised. 'How about you?'

'I'm a dancer,' he said.

'I thought maybe you were.'

'What makes you say that?'

'You have really nice posture,' I said. He pulled a confused face.

'What a lovely thing to say.' We stood there in silence for a moment. 'So you and the owner of the flat next door, she's your . . . friend?' He raised an eyebrow theatrically, I snorted and started laughing. 'I'm sorry!' he said. 'I didn't know how to ask.'

'No,' I replied, 'it's fine, you didn't know, Helene and I are together.'

'Okay, phew, I thought so. Anthony and I are also an item.' As soon as he mentioned Anthony his voice veered back into the mannered way of speaking he'd used initially. Every letter in his name was pronounced.

'How did you meet?' I said, unsure of their dynamic, unsure of what to ask.

'He came to see one of the shows I was dancing in, he waited for me by the stage door, isn't that romantic?' I agreed that it was romantic. I imagined what it would be like to watch Oliver dance from the heavy darkness of the theatre audience and I understood the impulse to wait around afterwards. He was very striking but more than that, he radiated warmth. I looked around the room.

'That's an amazing painting.' It was a dark still life, laid on thick with oil paint, the glittering centre of a pomegranate looked like it had been rendered in clotted blood.

'Anthony likes to collect things, you should see what he has in the other room.' Oliver pushed open the double doors and I peered inside. The living room was full of portraits, many of them nudes of handsome young men. Most of them stood against dark backgrounds, almost in chiaroscuro. All the paintings were vast, practically life-size, it was like standing in a room full of corpses.

'Wow,' I said.

'I know,' Oliver said, looking around as if he was seeing them for the first time. 'Sometimes I feel like I'm in competition with them, all these sexy men.' He laughed a short uncomfortable laugh at the end of the sentence, I knew he was admitting something true. I looked at him and he looked at me. There was an ease between us very quickly, it felt so good to be trusted, confided in. *We're both trespassers in these houses*, I thought, *you and I are the same.*

'What does Helene do?' he asked

'She works in an art gallery,' I said.

'Weird,' he said, 'that we've both ended up with arty people.' I skated over the assumption that I had *ended up* with Helene.

'Well, aren't you an artist?' He pulled a confused face. 'You're a dancer!' I said.

'Oh, I guess,' he said. 'My mum put me in ballroom dancing lessons when I was a kid because it was an after-school thing that was free, they needed a boy.' He frowned self-consciously and I laughed imagining poor Oliver practising with all his different partners, lifting one girl after the other.

There was a sharp loud sound like a stone hitting the window. I jumped and let out a little shriek.

'It's okay,' he said, 'don't worry!' He moved closer to the window and opened it to check what had made the noise. 'It's just a bird.' I went over to where he was standing.

'Don't look,' he said, but I peered through the window, there was a blue tit, stone-dead under the windowsill.

'It's completely dead,' I said. I was suddenly worried, what if the crockery started breaking over here too. I withdrew from the windowsill.

'I should probably go,' I said, patting my pockets for my things, but there was nothing there. I went back into the kitchen to look for my keys and my phone but they weren't there either.

'Oh, okay,' Oliver was saying as I searched around frantically.

'Did I have a phone and keys with me when I came in here?' He paused.

'I'm sorry, no, I don't think you did.' I panicked, I had no way of getting back into the house.

'I'm just going to go outside and check that I didn't drop them.' Oliver followed me outside and helped me look but there was nothing there. We looked through the window of Helene's flat and my keys and phone were plainly visible on the kitchen table.

'There's no spare key?' he asked.

'That was the spare key,' I said miserably.

'Well, come back inside, you can wait here until she comes home.'

'Are you sure?' I said, shivering violently.

'You don't really have any other option, do you?' He laughed and I laughed a bit too. He made us a second cup of coffee and talked to me about his childhood, the ballroom dancing, the spray tans, the glittering shirts. I relaxed into the sofa, it was extremely comfortable. At lunchtime he ordered us expensive burgers with Anthony's credit card. Unlike Helene, Anthony didn't just own a flat in the building, the whole house belonged to him, there were all these different floors.

'Technically, he has a title,' Oliver said as he showed me the upstairs.

'Really? What is it?'

'I don't even know, he's a baron or a lord or something.'

'Fucking hell,' I said. We looked at more of Anthony's paintings, Duncan Grants, Jean Cocteau drawings.

'All this beauty,' I said, 'and it's shut away in his house.'

'Tell me about it,' Oliver said, posing artfully in front of a gilt mirror, his hands framing his face, I laughed. He looked into one of the many clocks that adorned the second living room.

'It's after five. Drink?' I did a mental calculation, Helene had her cookery lesson, she would be home in around an hour and a half.

'That sounds amazing.' Oliver made us Manhattans using a drinks cart in Anthony's downstairs living room.

I sipped the drink and let it calm me. It was already dark outside. Oliver pushed the light switches and a soft glow emanated from a chandelier overhead. We drank two Manhattans each without making a dent in the contents of the shaker. Oliver connected his phone to some hidden speakers and put on a rowdy pop album. We shimmied and twirled. Oliver moved himself expertly as I shook my hair and wiggled my hips around. He laughed watching me trying to dance, he caught my hand and pulled me close into a ballroom stance.

'Don't worry,' he said, 'it's easy.' He showed me a waltz, turning and turning until we whirled around the carpet. I laughed aloud at the feeling. *I'm having a good time*, I thought to myself, *I feel safe here*. For the first time in months I felt genuinely carefree, and then all of a sudden the lights shut off.

'Oh no,' Oliver said into the darkness. 'That's the second time recently! Come on, let's go and look at the fuse box.' He took my hand and pulled me along with him, using the light on his phone to illuminate the way. I could smell the dust and the damp. Oliver examined the fuse box as I looked out into the dark basement. Slowly, imperceptibly, a shape started to move in the darkness, at first I thought it was writhing, then as my eyes adjusted to the dark I could see there was a figure moving towards us, closer and closer.

'Oliver,' I said. 'Oliver, can we go back upstairs?' I tried to control my voice.

'Are you scared of the dark?' he said jokingly as he scrutinised the fuse box. 'I think if I flip this switch then everything will be fine.' I heard a click but nothing happened, the darkness remained. 'Well that didn't work,' he muttered.

'Oliver,' I said, the figure was closer to us now, turning its head to the side, looking at me. I could almost recognise her. I gripped Oliver's hand. He looked at my face.

'Okay,' he said, 'let's go back to the living room.' We went back up the stairs and I let go of his hand, self-conscious about how sweaty I was. I felt itchy, like my arms and legs were covered in dust.

'Don't worry,' he said, 'we've got a ton of candles.' He extracted a box of matches and a fistful of candles from a drawer. He went around lighting them, a candelabra on the table, a series of pillar candles on the other surfaces. The effect was comforting and strange, like the moment at someone else's birthday party where the lights are out and you are about to start singing. We sat back down on the sofa, we sat cross-legged. We stared at each other.

'I've had a really fun day,' I said, 'even though everything went wrong.'

'Really?' Oliver grinned. 'Well, I'm glad. You can come over any time, if you're bored.' I smiled a little sadly and thought of Helene. I wondered where I would be in a month, a year.

'I don't really know how long I'll be here for.' There was a pause.

'I know what you mean,' he said. My chest hurt a little, *What are we doing with ourselves?* I thought. In my peripheral vision, a candle blew out. I turned to look at it and the smoke streamed out towards the ceiling.

'How did you do that?' Oliver said.

'I didn't do that,' I said.

'No, seriously.' He smiled. 'How'd you do that?' I shrugged. I thought about Helene again. I thought about the curve of her neck. A candle behind Oliver's head snuffed out. He turned to look then looked back at me. I thought about her and the man from the party. I thought of a picture I'd seen of the two of them together, they were both wearing the same kind of Italian sunglasses, his arm slung around her waist. A candle on the side table right next to Oliver snuffed out. He let out a gasp and I laughed. I looked up and I saw something by the door. The figure from the basement was moving closer to us in the dark. I tried to identify her features but I couldn't quite make them out. I could only just see where her face was supposed to be, her neck, her shoulders. The edges were fuzzy in the dark. The figure was standing behind Oliver. Then she perched on the sofa next to him, her body slumping against his shoulder, sinking deeper and deeper like she was made of melting wax.

There was a sharp tap on the window and we both jumped. It was Helene, she looked furious. I stood up immediately and looked around for my shoes. She walked around to the front door and rang the incredibly loud door-bell. I pulled the door open and she walked inside, breezing past me, already mid-sentence.

'So this is where you've been all day,' she said. 'Why all the *atmosphere*?' she said, gesturing at the candles.

'We had a blackout. We were waiting for the lights to come back on.'

'We've had those too,' Helene said, looking at me.

'I locked my phone and keys inside the house,' I explained, 'Oliver said I could stay here until you got home.'

'I'm Oliver,' he said, helpfully raising a hand.

'Helene,' she said back, without taking her hand out of her pocket to shake his like she did with everyone else that she met. 'I brought dinner home with me,' she said, already walking back towards the door. I stood up to follow her but walked over to Oliver first.

'Thank you so much for looking after me today,' I said. He took my hands in his.

'No problem, any time, I mean it,' he said.

'Are you coming?' Helene said from the corridor.

'Yes!' I called back, Oliver looked at me sympathetically and let go. I followed her out of the house and back into her flat, as soon as the door closed behind us I noticed Helene staring at me.

'That was really rude,' I said. 'It was really nice of him to let me stay there, I would have been stranded otherwise.'

'Yeah I bet he was so nice to you,' she replied as she took off her coat.

'Why are you jealous?' I asked, she was quiet and sarcastic and the alcohol was making my sentences loud and unwieldy.

'Oh I don't know? Maybe because I came home to you sitting in candlelight with a man you don't know.'

'He's obviously gay.'

'Oh you know exactly how gay everyone is all the time, do you?'

'No, not necessarily, I just felt safe I guess,' I said, suddenly embarrassed. She stepped towards me, she put her hand on the back of my neck. I thought she was trying to say something serious but instead she grabbed a fistful of my hair.

'Ow!' I said, my head jerked back.

'Don't do that again,' she said quietly.

'Helene, you're hurting me,' I said, she let go and laughed.

'You're so dramatic,' she said. She went back to extracting plates from the dresser and slamming them down on the counter, opening and shutting the cutlery drawer. The noise grated on me, I hated loud sudden noises, she knew that. I opened my mouth to say something about how the way she'd reacted was so unfair, so uncalled for, when she let out a shriek. She darted out of the way just in time as her dresser, slowly then all at once, keeled over onto the kitchen floor. It narrowly missed me too, I was a few inches away from the top of it, I'd watched it fall, frozen in horror as Helene cowered next to it.

'Oh my God,' she said, 'oh my God, what the hell?' I didn't know what to do, I looked down and my feet were covered in fragments of glass and porcelain plates.

'All my mother's plates smashed to pieces,' she said, dead-eyed.

'Helene,' I said, I didn't want to move. She stepped around the dresser to where I was standing.

'You're bleeding,' she said tenderly, 'step back, carefully.' I moved away from the dresser and that's when I felt the pain of it, several deep cuts on my ankles and feet, blood flowering through my socks.

'Ow,' I said, then as I started to cry, I said it again. 'OW.'

'Sit down,' she ordered me, 'stay there, I'll be right back.' I collapsed backwards onto a chair, I swung my legs up and rested them gingerly on an opposite chair. Helene returned with a bundle of tissue and a first-aid kit.

'I'm going to take these socks off now,' she said.

'No,' I said, 'please don't.' She ignored me, moving carefully and quickly, she eased them off my feet while I bit into the side of my hand.

'See. That wasn't so bad.' She quickly wiped them over with TCP as I made pathetic little hurt noises. She checked for excess shards, I was lucky there were none. I was certain

Helene would have insisted on pulling them out. After she'd disinfected my cuts she bound them up with gauze and little pieces of surgical tape.

'None of these cuts is particularly deep,' she said, 'you were lucky.' She looked back at me, she reached over and touched my face. I flinched and she looked hurt, but she didn't move her hand. I thought I could feel a smudge of blood transfer from her hand to my face but I didn't say anything. She licked her thumb and removed the smudge, then licked the blood back from her thumb.

*

I had to go into work the following evening, we bound up my feet with even more gauze but I could still feel the cuts as I walked around. I hobbled around the kitchen and restaurant, usually at work I rushed, worried everyone thought I was too slow, but now I had no choice but to slow down and no one seemed to notice or care. I was exhausted from the fight with Helene. I felt emotionally fragile, the way I did after a serious hangover. The heat of the kitchen was lulling me into a deep sleep. I looked around for something to keep myself awake. I wouldn't be able to make a coffee without drawing too much attention to myself. I checked no one was looking at me, then plucked two brown sugar cubes from a porcelain cup and popped them into my mouth. I crunched them then pushed the sediment around with my tongue until it had dissolved enough that I could swallow it. I instantly felt better, more alert. I had stopped dreaming about work but now work felt like a dream, there were long stretches where I spoke to no one. I couldn't remember the manager's name that shift, but he couldn't remember mine either. He waved a pointed finger at me, looking for my name tag, which I'd whipped into a skip outside the same night they'd given it to me.

'Hey, you,' he said weakly, he sounded exhausted.

'We don't really need you tonight. There's not enough reservations, why don't you go home?'

'Really? Great!' I said before he had the chance to answer. I seized my bag and coat from the hook and strode out before anyone could stop me.

*

When I got back to the flat I walked up to the door, I assumed Helene was inside, the lights in the kitchen were all on. I unlocked the door and walked in. I called out to her a few times, but the place felt empty. The kitchen was in disarray, several drawers and cupboards were open, I went around closing them. Her cupboard where she kept spare bottles of wine was wide open and it looked as if two were missing. I went into the bedroom but she wasn't in there either. I stood in the hallway chewing my lip.

I took out my phone and texted Helene **They let me go early, where are you?** I watched the little dots as she typed. **That's great** she said, **meet me here.** She sent me a location, a little pin dropped on a map. **Where are we going?** I asked, but she didn't respond.

I took a bus part of the way, the pin was next to a large expanse of green, a park I didn't recognise. I began walking in one direction then realised I was going the wrong way and turned to the left. I was looking down a dark alleyway with a single streetlight towards the end of it. It looked like a shortcut, I took a few steps down it. I started to shiver violently, the walls of the alleyway were so narrow, it was like the cold air was trapped. I felt a strange prickling feeling, like there was someone standing over my shoulder.

'You should leave.' I whipped my head around, there was a woman standing there looking at me. My heart beat faster and faster, though I was standing perfectly still. She was only a few paces away but her features were somehow unclear, unrecognisable. Her hair sat flatly around her face, it seemed dirty, stuck down on her neck. She seemed familiar, I had seen her before but I didn't know where. She didn't seem angry, or agitated, just tired.

'You shouldn't be here. It's not the right place.' I realised she was looking in my direction, but not completely at me. Her eyes were pale, vacant and blank. I thought maybe I'd wandered down a private road.

'I'm sorry. I didn't know,' I said, beginning to turn away from her and back towards the street, I could feel my sweat, slick under my clothes, and the cold air on my forehead.

'I know,' she said simply, 'there's no way you could have known. But you know now, you can leave, so you should leave.' She didn't move or point towards the right way to go. I felt that she was waiting for an answer.

'You're right. I'm going to leave. I'm leaving.' I backed away from her, when I turned around I heard her voice.

'Good.' She said then after a moment, 'Take care.' I paused, but something told me not to turn around. I walked back the way I came until I reached the main road, then I walked as fast as I could towards Helene's pin.

*

When I got there she was leaning against the railing and fidgeting, kicking one of her heels against the pavement, the knocking sound grated on my nerves.

'Hello,' I said warily, she stepped forward and kissed me, putting her hand on the back of my skull, I felt her tongue in my mouth. I pulled away before she did, I glimpsed her briefly, her eyes closed, her eyelashes twitching before her eyes opened. I thought, as I always did when I caught her off guard like this, of a painting of a saint depicted in spiritual ecstasy. She had that look. She adjusted the straps of her tote bag and it clinked, I could see bottles of wine poking out of the top.

'Where are we going?' I said. There wasn't anything around us except the park and houses, rows and rows of them in every direction.

'Let's go, you'll see once we get closer.' She moved a few steps in front of me then beckoned me again.

'Come on!' She said it playfully, like she was beckoning a child or a dog. I followed her anyway. I was certain I wasn't going to like where she was leading me. My heart thudded hard in my chest. She slid her hand down my forearm then laced her fingers with mine, holding my hand tight. Her hands were always so cold. She was smiling, swinging our hands as we walked. We walked deeper and deeper into the residential streets, they seemed even quieter than usual, almost all of the windows were dark. Her grip on my hand was starting to hurt, I tried to pull away but she only gripped it tighter.

'Helene,' I said, she seemed not to hear me. 'Helene! Let go please, you're hurting me.' She stopped to look at me reproachfully and dropped my hand. She shoved her hands in the pockets of her coat, the smile returning to her face, she cocked her head to one side.

'Do you know where we are right now?'

'No,' I said, I was cold.

'Look around, think about it.' I looked around, it did all look familiar. Like somewhere I had been in a dream, or somewhere I had stumbled through one night while very drunk. I felt a hot prickle of dread on the back of my neck. Helene smiled slightly and started walking again. We were at the top of a street, I stopped her outside one house, the windows glowed faintly orange through the curtains. She was striding ahead of me, she was going up the steps to the front door, I had to reach out to grab her skinny arm.

'Helene!' She turned to look at me, her pupils were huge, I could feel how tense she was, she was like a cat with all its fur standing up on end, I let go immediately.

'Is this his house?' I asked, I was completely certain that it was, but I needed her to confirm it, I needed her to say it. She grinned and a chill passed right through me, I could sense her excitement, it was panicked and sexual.

'Yes it is.' I put my hand to my mouth. I thought I would scream but I didn't, I didn't feel sad or betrayed, I felt only terror.

'What is it?' she said, she was mocking me. 'Don't you want him dead?' I felt the horrible sliding dread of someone being told something they already knew. I knew she wanted this, I knew she thought I wanted this, so why did I come? I think I had thought that this moment would never arrive, or that when it did I would want it, I would need to do it, I would feel what Helene was feeling, that manic desire to cover something in petrol and burn it to the ground. I didn't feel anything like that, I was frightened, I wanted to go home.

'I'm not going in there with you,' I said, before I could stop myself. 'I'm going home, I'm going back to my flat.'

141

For one crazy second I thought she was going to hit me. A muscle moved in her jaw.

'You can't make me go in there alone.' Her voice was quiet and toneless, we stared at each other, I always wanted her so much. I stayed where I was.

'I can't do it,' I said, it was as if saying it made it true. I felt it in my bones, it didn't matter what Helene said to me, I was never going to go back into that house, I was never going back to her house either, it was time for me to take myself home.

'Don't you understand?' she said, stepping towards me, she sounded emotional. 'It has to be you that does it.' *Why*, I thought to myself, *why on earth does it have to be me?*

'I want to watch. I want to watch you and then I want to clean up.' *No.* It was all completely wrong. She stepped towards me and I stepped back, I could feel it then, the way I was being pulled along. She watched the fear cross my face, the flinch as she tried to touch me.

'Let me go then, if you *can't*.' She looked at me then, hard. I had the strange sense that I knew exactly what she was feeling. She wasn't disappointed in me, she wasn't scared of what would happen if she went there alone. She wasn't sad because I was leaving her, she was furious because I was chickening out. I tried to say that I was sorry but I couldn't, the words wouldn't come out of my mouth. She looked at me hatefully then turned her head and spat in the street, it was a gesture that was bizarre, so totally out of character that I let out a nervous laugh. Before she could say anything else I turned around and started to walk, fast, in the direction of the way we had come. I could hear the sound of her voice but not what she was saying, she was stage whispering, then talking loudly, then shouting. I walked as fast as I could without breaking into a run. I looked back, only once, from a safe distance, but she had already gone inside.

Epilogue

She might have got away with it if she'd been less vengeful in her approach. She wanted to make me look at what she'd done, what she thought was the only thing to do.

*

The package was about the size of a side of beef, it was wrapped in so much transparent plastic it was almost white and it was bound around the middle several times with silver duct tape. On the top a piece of paper was taped to it with my name and address on it in permanent marker cursive. After everything, I had gone back to my old bedsit. Once I knew what the alternative was, I didn't dislike it so much anymore. There was no postage on it, it was made to look like a parcel that had been delivered in the usual way but I knew what it was and where it had come from immediately. I stood in the doorway staring at it, clutching at the door frame like I was afraid I would fall if I let go.

I was sitting on the curb when the police arrived, a few steps away from the package, staring at it like it was my opponent in a game of chess. They started laughing when they saw me.

*

I was terrified they'd lock me up for it. I puked at the sight of his hacked-up body, which helped. Then at the police station I passed out, theatrically, my eyes rolling back in my head like a cartoon. No one could say I wasn't in shock. They wanted every single detail. I kept the haunting stuff to myself. Hours into the interrogation, once we got to the end of my explanation of what had happened that night as we fought outside his house, I succumbed to the weight of everything that had happened. I broke down in great heaving sobs, I stretched my arms out and grabbed the edge of the table, I rested my head on my parallel arms and wept. I did this for a few minutes before the sound of my own misery began to make me self-conscious, I sounded like a tortured animal.

*

I felt certain they wouldn't believe me, about the man from the party, about Helene. I thought about Helene's demeanour, how quiet she could seem, how calm, how I was permanently fidgeting next to her, always laughing nervously.

*

Helene looked sullen in court, she slumped down in her chair, she contemplated her split ends. They produced, I don't know how, messages she had sent to the man while I had been living with her. I couldn't even recognise her voice in them, they were flirtatious, affectionate, I couldn't bear it, they called each other *baby*. When they turned sexual I clamped my hands forcefully over my ears and put my head between my knees until it was over. On the way out, among the crush of press photographers, she wore huge Jackie O sunglasses that obscured her face. I thought it was a nice touch. I never saw her whole face in real life again, not once did she turn her head to look at me.

*

I heard that on the stand his mother blubbered about what a sweet boy he was, about how much he loved her, how he sent her flowers on her birthday. I had to remind myself from time to time that in spite of everything, I didn't really think he deserved to die.

*

I didn't forgive him. There wasn't anything unusual about him, he wasn't good, maybe he wasn't redeemable. He would always be there, or men like him would; without some massive act of God they would carry on hurting us, and the earth would continue to be covered in our ghosts. I would have to learn to live with my anger, I could feel it was going to go on forever. I could feel it churning and

147

reproducing inside me like heat, rising out of me and dissolving as it got further away from me, its source, a white dwarf burning into the dark.

*

My life continued. In the end, I wanted to stay in the flat but I couldn't. I got a different job, I moved all the way across town. I found ways to feel different. I did things like rearranging my furniture to make the flat easier to live in, I bought a chair off the internet, I cooked and slept.

*

Helene is still in prison. I imagine she's doing exceptionally well. She has the kind of personality where she's incapable of failure. She's not subject to fate or circumstances like the rest of us, she'll always find a way to do what she is going to do. I've looked at the theories online, there's a small but vocal contingent of people who are convinced that I masterminded the whole mess. One of them uploaded pictures of Helene's and my arms in a side-by-side comparison. *Which one do you REALLY think could lift a whole grown man's body??* Someone replied: *That's not muscle it's FAT* and I laughed aloud. Helene's arms do look especially birdlike in the photo they chose. A few different users have tried to explain that none of my DNA was at the scene but it doesn't seem to make any difference to the amateur detectives. They're convinced of my guilt, that all the manipulation was the other way around. They'd try and find me if they could. I was even given two new names. I like them more than my old ones, I don't even answer to the old ones anymore, these days I could be anyone.

Acknowledgements

Firstly, I am deeply indebted to Daisy Chandley, my wonderful agent, whose unfailing belief in me and this book has magicked it into existence. I wish to thank Peters Fraser and Dunlop agents, particularly for their Queer Fiction Prize, and for shortlisting me.

I would like to express my utmost thanks to the whole team at Sceptre. In particular my editors: Ansa Khan Khattak, Nico Parfitt and Jo Dingley, without whom this book would be bad.

I would like to thank Manor House Library and the volunteers who keep it open, for providing a place to write.

I would like to thank Samuel Gormley, for the full stops, and Jack Wrighton, for taking several good pictures of me.

Endless thanks is due to my family for their unfailing support.

Lastly I would like to thank the following people for being that essential combination of friend and reader: Catriona Bolt, Alexander Hartley, Cat Madden, Alastair Curtis and Emily Meller.